Lost American Fiction

EDITED BY Matthew J. Bruccoli

The title for this series, Lost American Fiction, is
unsatisfactory. A more accurate series title would
be "Forgotten American Works of Fiction That
Deserve a New Public"—which states the rationale
for reprinting these titles. No claim is made that
we are resuscitating lost masterpieces, although the
first work in the series, Edith Summers Kelley's
Weeds, may qualify. We are simply reprinting
some works that are worth rereading because they
are now social documents *(Dry Martini)* or literary
documents *(The Professors Like Vodka)*. It isn't
that simple, for Southern Illinois University Press
is a scholarly publisher; and we do have serious
ambitions for the series. We expect that these titles
will revive some books and authors from un-
deserved obscurity, and that the series will there-
fore plug some of the holes in American literary
history. Of course, we hope to find an occasional
lost masterpiece.

M. J. B.

JOHN THOMAS

DRY MARTINI:

A Gentleman Turns to Love

With an Afterword
By Morrill Cody

SOUTHERN ILLINOIS UNIVERSITY PRESS
Carbondale and Edwardsville

Feffer & Sons, Inc.
London and Amsterdam

Library of Congress Cataloging in Publication Data
Thomas, John, 1900-1932.
    Dry martini: a gentleman turns to love.
    (Lost American fiction)
    Reprint of the ed. published by G. H. Doran Co., New York, with
an afterword.
    I. Title.
PZ3.T3637Dr9   [PS3539.H5874]   813'.5'2   73-14675
ISBN 0-8093-0661-1

Copyright 1926 by George H. Doran Company
Afterword by *Morrill Cody* and Textual Note by *Matthew J. Bruccoli,*
    copyright © 1974 by Southern Illinois University Press
All rights reserved
This edition printed by offset lithography in the United States of
    America
Designed by Gary Gore

TO MY FATHER

CONTENTS

vii

CONTENTS

DRY MARTINI

DRY MARTINI:

A Gentleman Turns to Love

CHAPTER 1.

Disquisition Anent the Alcoholic Content of Paris.

THERE was a day—yet fresh in the minds of the reminiscent—when the cocktail as an institution was a firm block in the foundation of the traveling American's nostalgia. Paris was to the thirsty exile a desert of quaint pink extracts, innocuous wines, nauseous liqueurs, disappointing cognacs, and inadequate beers. The strong waters of the Anglo-Saxon were to be uncovered only after the recondite investigation of the practiced explorer.

Toward the close of the second decade

of the twentieth century, however, there
appeared in France a group of gallant
adventurers collectively known by the
cryptic letters "A. E. F." They proved,
to the startled alarm of the native Gaul,
merely the vanguard of a hectic stam-
pede of tall Nordic tourists, driven by
that great, elemental impulse to race
migration—drought.

Right and left over the fair city by the
Seine they sowed the hardy Martini, the
fruitful Bronx, the sturdy Manhattan,
the rugged highball. And Paris proved
fertile ground. From the broad plateau
of the Place de la Concorde to the pleasant slopes of Montmartre flourished the
fruit of their sowing. Bar after bar
sprang like alcoholic mushrooms among
the drab cafés, and from each bar new
refugees from the parched Americas
plucked their drinks and scattered them
anew over the city of rambling streets
and unending laughter. So that there
was no end to the succession of bars and
barrooms, and to the quiet sun of France
arose the fuming incense of whisky and

gin in a thousand forms and a thousand blends.

Now, of all the gleaming dispensaries of merriment, the most renowned, at the time of our contemplation, was the momentous establishment on the rue Duphot, over whose swinging portals hung a large illuminated sign proclaiming it as the "Garden of Allah," but known to the initiate more simply as "Dan's place." Why the thirsty expatriate should have found more joy with his foot upon the particular brass rail adorning Dan's bar than upon many another identical rail is a problem which may never be adequately solved. The fact that its clientèle was exclusively male, that the tables invitingly scattered about the room were unadorned by the frail exponents of professional complaisance, elsewhere omnipresent, may have had a little to do with it. The immaculate utensils, polished mirror, glistening mahogany were doubtless all factors in its triumph. Prompt and skilled service played its part. Most of all, the personality of the inimitable

Dan drew to him his "clients" as by a gigantic lodestone.

Dan was a large Irishman with a ruddy face and a chuckling laugh which scattered animosity before it. It were too massive an endeavor to try to dissect here the mysterious quality which distinguishes the great bartender from the lesser of his kind. Long evenings have been passed in the fragrant stuffiness of countless saloons in fruitless, endless discussion of that same fascinating topic. The merits of this one and of that one—the tact of Sam and the wit of Alf, the tolerance of Joe and the intolerance of George, the courtesy of Frank and the kindliness of Jim—have been weighed and contemplated and related until the accents of the speakers blur into a gymnastic tangling of tongues. Enough to admit the fact—Dan was the greatest barman of his day in Paris. In his transmuting hands a cocktail took on new flavors and new glories. Under his soothing tones the most belligerent of militant

14

imbibers were calmed to amiable tractability. He was at once father, servant, confessor, friend and adviser to his appreciative clientèle.

And of all the frequenters of Dan's place the most frequent and valued was without doubt my very good friend, Mr. Willoughby Quimby. There are many Willoughby Quimbys in the world— more than the world is aware of. They are to be seen on Broadway and Piccadilly, on the Promenade des Anglais and on the Lido, but wherever else they may roam, they find their occasional way to Paris—and to Dan's place.

Mr. Willoughby Quimby, to be precise, belonged to that class of mankind known variously as "men of the world," "high livers," "parasites," "epicures," and "drunkards." His male acquaintances were of the barrooms, his occupation was the conscientious evasion of responsibility.

Mr. Quimby, after the fashion of his kind, presented a flawless exterior to the

world he lived in. There was no gap in
the armor of his *savoir faire*. His manner, in the most critical periods, was as
impeccable as his attire. His dissipations
were conducted as the debauchery of a
gentleman should be conducted. He was
contemplated with reverent awe by the
aspiring young-men-about-town. His
life in Paris was complete and self-con-
tained. It bore no relationship to the
progress of the world. He went from
bar to bar, from cabaret to cabaret, and
he faced every problem of life with a
suave negation which made his position
impregnable.

And under the shell of his manner?
Mr. Quimby, it must be assumed, was
human. And humanity is not only a manner, not merely a concealment. So we
may glance at the garnered facts of a
climactic period in the life of Willoughby
Quimby and permit ourselves to specu-
late upon the very human man under the
manner and see just how impregnable
after all is the armor of urbanity.

The crisis dates from the morning when Willoughby Quimby's mail contained two letters, neither of them of an accustomed nature.

CHAPTER 2.

Letters.

MY DEAR FATHER:

You will be astonished no doubt and gratified conceivably to learn that your prodigal daughter is returning to the—I am told—none too domestic paternal hearth. I should, in fact, be in Paris almost as soon as this letter. Arriving, that is, on the *Parenthetic,* May fifteenth. Please take all requisite steps to insure the comparative reputability of your household. I have been insufferably well brought up by Mother—your wife—you recall—and a too sudden tumble from the pinnacles of respectability might unnerve me.

Mother would doubtless join me in sending our dearest love, except that at present writing Mother has the same degree of fondness for both of us as for the local rattler.

Meanwhile, you will have to take me on faith—and for an indefinite period—as your affectionate, if not particularly dutiful daughter,

Elizabeth.

P. S. In case you don't know, I am twenty years old and not at all bad looking.—E.

P. S. For heaven's sake, don't kill the fatted calf. I loathe veal.—E.

P. S. They tell me you are fat, fast, and foppish. Are you?—E.

DARLING WILLOUGHBY:

By the time you receive this you will undoubtedly have seen or heard from the young phenomenon who owes her existence to our regrettable coöperation. I have been trying over a period of years to stifle my conscience sufficiently to wash my hands of her and ship her to you, for better or (more probably) worse.

Finally, the problem has solved itself. She has, with some semblance of resolution, washed her hands of me.

You have been good enough—through the worst motives—to leave her upbringing until the present time entirely to me, and I may be permitted to assure you that it has been no light task. The child takes after both of us. She is incorrigibly stubborn, willful, immoral, eccentric, temperamental. I have ruled her with an elephant goad, the iron rod having been previously hopelessly bent on her admirably shaped skull. I have contrived to keep her in the most superbly patrician isolation. Theoretically, the world and its ways are a tightly closed book to our little one. Practically, her wisdom of it appears to be boundless. My treatment of her case seems to be a failure. Now you can see what you can do!

I am reliably informed that you drink constantly, that you persist in your other less ostensible forms of indulgence, and that you are beginning to lose your hair. The fact that you are clearly the most ideally unsuitable individual to place in charge of a budding daughter gives me some hope. You may be precisely the form of medicine required by our unhappy offspring. In any case, I am left no choice. The brat insists on going to you.

She will be chaperoned as far as Paris by one Miss Whittlesey, a teacher at the school from which she was last dismissed. For further information, I can only refer you to the excellent Miss Whittlesey. Don't look for any advice from me. I leave you to your conscience.

As for myself, I am unfortunately unchanged and plan to remarry as soon as practicable. I may find it necessary to come to Paris to do it. Don't be alarmed, though. I'll give you plenty of time to accustom yourself to fatherhood before I intrude on your menage.

How have you been for the last twelve years?

Affectionately,

Florence.

CHAPTER 3.

Mr. Willoughby Quimby Undertakes to Put His House in Order.

"WHISKY-SODA?"

Her tone implied rather a ritual than an interrogation. But he brushed the remark impatiently aside, rumpling his ever so slightly grizzled hair with one nervous hand, while he bit, with varying degrees of success, at the fringe of his ever so slightly dyed mustache.

"Whisky and soda!" he wailed dismally. "Whisky and soda! I indicate to you the complete and irremediable dissolution of my life, my career, its significance, its ideals—and you dare to talk to me of whisky! Georgette, Georgette! I begin to think that I have been deceived in you. You are, I am convinced, of all

22

my mistresses the most callous, the least considerate. And when I think——!"

Georgette, however, the little composed smile unchanged on her lips, proceeded to fill a generous half-tumbler from a cut-glass decanter. One hand, meanwhile, disposed the folds of her thin silk dressing gown in such fashion as discreetly to display the soft excellence of her body. Georgette was young, undeniably young, but life had not failed to add to her innate Gallic sense of the logic in things and people a plenteous seasoning of wisdom of the world and the males who are its bankers. Her eyes, soft as moonlight and blue as the night, possessed a curiously aloof penetrative quality clothed in a caressing tenderness.

Mr. Willoughby Quimby took the glass distractedly, added a modicum of soda from the siphon at his elbow, and drank in quick, agitated gulps. His blue eyes blinked excitedly in their puffy sockets. Even his somewhat plump cheeks quivered a little. Mr. Quimby was disturbed.

Georgette seated herself on the arm of his chair and pinched his nose unconcernedly. It was an agreeable nose—not too aquiline—not quite too fleshy, and tinted to a convivial scarlet. Nevertheless, in his present mood, Mr. Quimby resented having it toyed with. He brushed the neatly manicured little fingers away in some indignation. Then, repenting of the gesture, he placed a contrite arm about Georgette's waist and drew her closer. She made pleasant, contented noises and her short curls tickled his forehead warmly.

"You can imagine, my little one," observed Mr. Quimby, more calmly, now (they were speaking French, partly because he spoke it almost perfectly, and, more particularly, because she spoke nothing else)—"you can imagine that it is not a pleasure for me to be in so disagreeable a mood. On the other hand, I pray you to bear in mind all that this catastrophe implies—all that it will mean to 'our relationship.' "

"But of course I understand! It is ap-

24

palling to have a child on one's hands!
I know, because so many of my friends
have had that impossible situation thrust
upon them. But why it should make a
difference to us—to our love—that, I con-
fess, I do not see."

Mr. Quimby was for a moment at a
loss. Passing a hand through his hair
with his accustomed nervous gesture, he
replied with a shade of annoyance:

"It makes just this difference: we are
finished! Through."

"*Comment*—finished?"

"Just that," went on Mr. Quimby, with
florid eloquence. "Do you think I can
lead a double life? Do you think I can
permit my little girl, the flower that is
to brighten my old age, to find out that
while I imprint the kiss of fatherly protection on her forehead, I am simultane-
ously thinking of the imminent dishonor-
able embraces of a——?"

He paused, a little disconcerted. After
all, a touch of diplomacy would perhaps
not be out of place. But Georgette gave

him no chance to resume. The blue eyes
were suddenly hard.

"You mean then—you in whom I have
trusted as in no other man—you mean
that you throw me out on the streets because of some miserable chit of a Yankee
daughter whom you have never even
seen?"

She leaped up furiously, her dressing
gown swishing about her tense form, and
stamped her slippered foot. Then she
paused, either because she had stubbed
her toe or because Mr. Quimby straightened himself up in his chair and his eyes
were bright with sudden and unexpected
fire. Also his hand was tugging furiously
at the graying hair. His voice shook
when he answered, but he did so with a
dignity not incompatible with his opulent
stomach and too impeccably tailored
clothing.

"You will be very kind, my dear
Georgette, not to refer again to my
daughter in those terms. If possible, do
not speak of her at all. As to the other
matter, you may be tranquil. You will

26

at least be materially provided for as
you have been in the past. It is only the
more intimate aspects of our association
which must be curtailed."

Whether due to the substance or the
manner of this observation, Georgette
was completely melted. She sank immediately to the footstool at his feet and the
blue eyes, luminous now and not very far
from his own, overwhelmed Mr. Quimby
with the assurance of her remorse, ad-
dressing him most endearingly as her
"little fat one," "her little cabbage," her
"naughty but adored one" and so on with
ever-waxing tenderness.

"How could you think," she re-
proached him gently, "that your little
Georgette could have so much as thought
of the money? You should know that
she would make any sacrifice for her
Willy's happiness—starve, if need be.
Besides, I was sure that you would pro-
vide for me, my dearest, even if fate
forced us apart. No; it is only the
thought that our love may be marred by

a third person that made me for a moment lose myself in a passion of terror."

Mr. Quimby leaned back in his chair again and lit a cigarette, thrusting his legs vaguely in the direction of a fire in the grate across the room. This was more like it. Georgette was a sweet girl. Particularly when you felt her little body pressing against your knees this way, and her two little hands fluttering timidly along your arms. Mr. Quimby almost forgot the catastrophe—forgot that these manifold charms were no longer to be his. Georgette's voice came to him softly, gratefully. Eyes half-closed, he looked speculatively down at her. There was something vital about Georgette. She was so rich and passionate in her beauty. He passed his hand affectionately along the electric softness of her arm, patted her shoulders lightly, and held her face between his two palms. She stopped talking and smiled a little— a smile whose warmth one actually felt. That was the thing about Georgette; she

28

was so warm, so understanding, so—
sympathique.

He came to himself with a jerk when
his cigarette tip burned his finger. After
all, he reflected in some dismay, the object of this visit was to bid Georgette
farewell forever. He rose hastily, almost
upsetting the girl at his feet. But she,
too, leaped up lightly, the smile of affection changing suddenly to a look of
troubled apprehension.

"What is it?"

"I must go," he snapped.

"Why?"

"You know why—please don't make
me repeat it. I must stay clean—for the
girl's sake."

"Clean? What is there unclean about
our love?"

This was not easy to answer, but Mr.
Quimby was firm.

"In the first place, it isn't love. You
know that."

Georgette looked up, and the blue of
her eyes deepened.

"Isn't it?" she asked naïvely.

He looked away hastily, and seized his hat and stick.

"I must go," he muttered.

She came very close, her two hands slipping up to his shoulders. He felt her slim, hardly clad body close to him. The scent of it, the delicate perfume was in his nostrils—he could have said, in his brain.

"Stay just once more," she murmured. "Just once more, and then—we will perhaps part—forever. Don't go now."

"I must go!" he growled, as the soft brown curls nestled into his shoulder. "I must go!"

Nevertheless, Mr. Quimby did not go.

CHAPTER 4.

Wherein Cocktails are Quantitatively Absorbed.

ON leaving Georgette, some two hours later, Willoughby Quimby paused to debate his next measure. The way must be cleared for the advent of his child. There must be no stone left unturned to insure her protection from the contamination of his rather unfortunate way of life. Who else, besides Georgette, he pondered, as he turned into the Avenue de l'Opéra, should be notified of the impending alteration in his conduct?

There, was to be sure, Giselle, the melancholy midinette hard by the Madeleine. Also there was Vivienne—shapely, vivacious little Vivienne—at the Casino de Paris. There were, he meditated shamefacedly, several Viviennes at the

Casino de Paris—or at the Marigny, or at the Ambassadeurs. On the whole, none of them seemed to present a serious obstacle to abrupt reform. Possibly, in the case of Vivienne, a visit, in passing, to Cartier's. Otherwise, Mr. Quimby felt that his past might quite readily be consigned to the past, and that the path of temperate righteousness lay broad and clear before him.

Thus relieved of concern for the relation of past with future, he turned his attention to the delectable present. It was six o'clock in the afternoon. It was Paris in May. All things were possible—perhaps excepting those things which might ordinarily have been uppermost in Willoughby Quimby's mind. He sighed deeply, turned instinctively to glance after a lovely face in a limousine window, collided with someone, raised his hat in apology, hailed a taxi from the rank down the middle of the street. Receiving only a disinterested stare from the chauffeur thereof, he crossed to the taxi, nimbly evading one pelting autobus,

one gliding Hispano-Suiza, and one jolt-
ing fiacre.

At seven-thirty Mr. Quimby was to
meet Freddy Fletcher at his (Mr.
Quimby's) rooms, with a view to cocktails and subsequent dinner. The inter-
vening hour and a half proved a problem
too knotty for complex solution. He cut
the knot, with almost a shudder at his
own weakness. His shame lasted
throughout the brief, wild dash in the
bounding taxi to the door of Dan's. He
hadn't meant to go to Dan's this evening,
he reflected gloomily. Why go to Dan's?
On the other hand, why not?

Once arrived, he paid the taxi driver
—like most taxi drivers, a Muscovite
nobleman—and walked disconsolately in.

Dan's was crowded. Dan's always was
crowded at six. There were rows of dev-
otees in varied stages of conviviality
gathered before the polished mahogany
altar behind which Dan and his white-
coated disciples dispensed fluid cheer.

Overhead, a blue cloud of smoke
drifted and swirled. An agreeable aroma

of tobacco and alcohol insidiously urged
the already eager thirst. Nor was the
sense of hearing neglected at Dan's. The
sound of ice, adeptly agitated in silver
containers; the gurgle of vari-tinted liquids from vari-shaped bottles; the inter-
mittent pop of a champagne cork; the
ordered clicking of poker dice; a babel
of congenial tongues.

Mr. Quimby paused thoughtfully to
contemplate the scene. He would have
liked less of a crowd. But they were a
nice crowd—the cream of drinking Paris.
There was always an agreeable atmosphere of bibulous aristocracy at Dan's.
Not that there were not interlopers—
transient intruders on the selected excellence of Dan's clientele. For it was, in
a sense, selected. Dan had a shrewd and
active eye and, though his courtesy never
failed in decorous deference, his favor
he bestowed not lightly and without it his
welcome had an unpropitious if indefinable chill.

Mr. Quimby perceived many of the
familiar faces. There was, for example,

34

old Laurence Murphy, big and affable,
retelling for the fiftieth time, to a new
audience, the somewhat doubtful anec-
dote which he alone knew how to tell
adequately. There was Marcel Fequier,
clad in the last foppish extreme, chiefly
known as the husband of Zarini, the
dancer. There were other husbands of
other women of note. There was Paul
Fisher, who was said to be the most brilliant newspaper correspondent in Europe, on the infrequent. occasions of his
being sober enough to write. There was
Ward Johnson, the young American with
some money and no occupation, who
came to Paris four years ago for a brief
visit and had never been able to stay out
of Dan's long enough to catch the boat
back. There was old Matthew Stone,
who spent all afternoon getting drunk
enough to speak, and all night getting
drunk enough not to be able to speak.
There was Amos Thornton, the million-
aire railroad magnate, in for his method-
ical two Martinis nightly. There was
Prince Raginoff, lion-headed old Rus-

sian, with the manner and the glance of empire and the pocket of poverty. There was Rene Perez, cosmopolitan gambler and crook, tall and polished and charming. Mr. Quimby knew them all—liked most of them. He even liked Joe Drake, the black-haired ex-jockey, who passed him on his way out with a bluff quip. He liked Conway Cross, over there, the handsome, philandering artist.

Mr. Quimby felt already gently exhilarated as he made his way finally to the bar, answered Dan's cheery smile and prompt "Good morning, Mr. Quimby!" and exchanged greetings with the bearded Marquis de Poplin, who stopped in habitually for a Dubonnet and a mildly supercilious glance around.

Mr. Quimby felt a hand on his arm and turned to meet the nervous, cheery glance of Tommy Sterling. Captain Thomas Sterling, "something at the British Embassy," was heir to various important things, including wealth. He was also one of those people whom you liked in spite of yourself and were in some queer way proud of yourself for liking.

"Have a drink?" proposed Tommy.

"You touch upon the thought at this moment uppermost in my mind," acknowledged Willoughby Quimby. "Dan!"

"The usual, Mr. Quimby?"

"A light one, Dan. A very light one."

Dan glanced at him sharply, and concluded to ignore the qualification. A bottle in each practiced hand, he poured the ingredients of the Martini into a high glass vessel half-filled with ice and applied himself to mingling them with violence. Thoughtfully Mr. Quimby toyed with his malacca stick, his pale blue gaze following the process disinterestedly. The gaze brightened perceptibly as the artist poured his creation, a fragrant amber, into the thin-stemmed glass.

"Tommy," said Mr. Quimby, moodily —"Tomorrow I shall have a daughter."

"Dear, dear!" sympathetically murmured Tommy.

"She is twenty years old."

"I beg your pardon?"

"But I haven't seen her for twelve years," continued Willoughby Quimby.

"Oh!"

"Tommy—what shall I do about it?"

Tommy reflected gravely and sought inspiration in his champagne cocktail.

"If I were you, I'd wait and see what she's like."

"I am going to stop drinking."

"Are you?"

"I assure you. And I am going to become very serious."

"Are you?"

"You don't believe me?"

"I feel for you. When does your metamorphosis take place?"

"It has already begun to take place. Tomorrow it becomes complete."

"In that case, I must insist on your intoxication at dinner tonight—at my place."

"You can't have it. I'm dining with Freddy Fletcher."

"Must you? Elaine and Roger will be in our party."

"Unhappily, I must even forego Elaine and Roger."

"Then join us after dinner. The Jardin —and then almost anything. A last fling before you become a family man—eh?"

Mr. Quimby's eye rested thoughtfully on Dan, skillful, ubiquitous, carrying on several simultaneous conversations with easy good humor. This was Dan's busy hour, and he rose to it with the vitality of genius. He was everywhere at once, his poise matchless, his disposition unruffled, his body tireless. Behind him his three assistants trotted busily back and forth, smashing glasses, dropping trays, all in the infallible assurance that not one of their blunders escaped their chief's alert eye.

"I suppose I might meet you then, Tommy. If I won't be intruding . . ."

"Rot. Can't afford to miss your last night of freedom. Child staying long?"

"Indefinitely. Another drink?"

"Silly question! The same, Dan."

Mr. Quimby sipped listlessly. His drink seemed to him tasteless, flat. He finished it finally with an impatient gulp, and turned to leave.

"You must meet my offspring some day, Tommy."

"Like to. Have a drink."

"No. No more. Got to start to get in training for the guidance of adolescent girlhood."

"Don't be absurd. Another Martini, Dan."

Mr. Quimby could have wept.

"Don't, Tommy! Please don't! I mustn't drink!" He was really pathetic about it. But the drink, when it came, cheered him up a little. And the next proved more cheering yet, so that he departed at about seven in a state of rare good humor toward Dan, Tommy and the world in general.

Also he had made a decision. He would enlist Tommy's services in the up-bringing of Elizabeth. No one could be more desirable—a better or wiser influence for budding womanhood.

CHAPTER 5.

*Effects the Presentation, in a Charac-
teristic Attitude, of Miss
Elizabeth Quimby.*

THEY had found an agreeably reticent
nook on the forward end of the *Parenthetic's* promenade deck. Over their
heads darkly hung the bridge. They
were seated on something vaguely nauti-
cal—possibly one of the numberless cas-
kets of rope strewn about the decks of
transatlantic liners. To their obscure
retreat penetrated not the faintest gleam
of the generously sprayed starlight.

Ahead of them they could see the ship's
bow stirring restlessly in the water. They
were not conscious of forward motion.
Only the great prow lifted a little and
fell a little; carelessly, mightily. They
could hear the faint swish of water, see

the long low swells move grandly
towards them, meet them, pass on to the
endless ocean behind. And the solitary
mast swayed just perceptibly against the
stars, powdered over the heavens. There
was, to starboard, the merest curved
peeling of a moon, a slim bright thing,
shining green among a thousand stars.

On the other hand, Elizabeth was quite
conscious of the fact that it was not particularly warm. She drew her thin cape
closer over her bare arms and shivered a
little. Almost she regretted having left
the smoking-room—caviar sandwiches,
champagne and all. But the fat gentleman with the elk's tooth—the typical
"life of the party" had been a little bit
too much! She winced at the thought of
that genial alcoholic group, drawn together under the spell of the youth from
Hawaii who played the ukelele. She
didn't dislike any of them individually.
The little poet who was always drunk
and a trifle goggle-eyed; the long slim
man with the sharp nose and the too-
ready wit; the plump man whose idea of

fun in some way involved recurrent convulsive attempts to hold her hand; the well-known boxer, complacent focus of a wide-eyed group of flappers; the well-known politician, waxing oratorical in his cups; the human rhinoceros who alternately wheezed and absorbed whisky; the lady with the important bosom, its charms candidly set forth by a purple décolleté; the pretty woman with the hard voice and the spiky eye-lashes, bibulously hearty between two ecstatic tired business-men;—they were all right, all of them. But Elizabeth was embarking on her great adventure, and there was nothing great or adventurous about this atmosphere of smoke and alcohol and sticky humor—no matter how quickly the empty champagne bottles accumulated.

But she could not go to her cabin. The impeccable Miss Whittlesey, even asleep, was a burden to the soaring imagination. Lucille Grosvenor, whose curiously subtle candor was surprisingly a solace, had gone down long ago. And Elizabeth

tonight feared to be alone with the ocean.
Her breaking of old ties had in it something terrifying. She did not quite know
what it was—this mystery of life that lay
before her. Only she knew that its implications, to her, were magic and inter-
minable. She did not dare to question
the misty future lying yonder under the
stars. Least of all did she want to be
questioned. She had no answers—and
she felt that the Atlantic might demand
answers.

Bobby Duncan's invitation had been a
straw to clutch. Bobby was a nice boy—
and she felt her power over him. He was
puzzled by her, which gave her a firm
base to stand on, gave her thoughts a
sort of purchase. Of course, Bobby had
had a lot to drink, but he would be all
right when the air struck him.

Bobby, meanwhile, was considerably
elated at being just where he was with
Elizabeth. The night and the mysteriously extended ocean and the silver-
strewn waves worked insidiously upon
him. He felt vaguely joyful—a mood

44

akin to, but different from his previous hilarious intoxication.

On the other hand, Elizabeth was hard to talk to. She always was a little. But tonight her mind seemed to set in curious ways. He essayed a few pleasantries, a few self-conscious banalities on the beauty of the night, and paused to ponder. Tentatively, he closed his hand over one of hers. After all, there were formulæ, there were established precedents. He must do that which was expected of him.

Awkwardly he dropped his right arm about her shoulders. She made no effort to avoid it. He drew it closer.

"Cold?" he mumbled solicitously.

"A little. How cold the moon must be!"

Bobby laughed politely and drew her gingerly to him.

"That better?"

"I suppose so."

Thereupon Bobby, with a somewhat complicated twisting of his body, contrived to get his left hand to her face and turned it up to his. She drew away impatiently. He drew her back again.

"Don't be silly, Bobby," she rebuked him.

"I'm not being silly!" was the indignant rejoinder. "Merely affectionate."

"It's much too cold for affection. Must you?"

Bobby, it appeared, must. At any rate he persisted clumsily until he had contrived to apply his lips to hers. They were disappointingly unresponsive, but Bobby felt called upon to exert himself. He didn't do things by halves. So he squeezed his companion and crushed her lips to his with a bold semblance of passion, with some difficulty restraining his teeth, the while, from chattering. Elizabeth was limp and acquiescent. She made no move. Finally Bobby's ardor began to cool. His posture was both cold and uncomfortable. And the kiss was a little long-drawn he felt. Yet he would not sacrifice his dignity by being the first to break away. It was his place to continue until the lady's feeble protests caused him reluctantly to desist. Meanwhile, the kiss went on.

Elizabeth finally took pity and pushed him gently away.

"You kiss too sweetly, Bobby!" she commented amiably.

They were silent for awhile, looking out over the ocean—a little constrained, both of them.

"Do you mind sitting out here, Bobby?" asked Elizabeth, finally. "You aren't too cold, are you?"

"Not a bit!" proclaimed Bobby bravely. "I think it's fine. Great sight, isn't it?" He indicated the Atlantic with a vague sweep of the arm.

"How do you feel about going to Paris—really?" went on the girl. There was always a half-frightened reverence in her voice when she referred to Paris. She might have been a pilgrim, speaking of Mecca.

"Feel about it?" puzzled Bobby. "Why —I don't know. I'm damn glad I'm going there, if that's what you mean."

She sighed wearily. If only there were

some one she could talk to, some one who could understand!

"I feel," she said, "as though I had suddenly sprouted wings. You don't know what this trip means to me. I've been going slowly mad for years—and now I'm suddenly free. I feel as if Paris represented everything that I've always longed for—mystery and beauty and—and—Passion."

Bobby wondered if this was a cue. He made an abortive attempt to resume the kissing of her, but found himself impatiently repulsed.

"Not now, Bobby. I want to talk about Paris—if you don't mind?" She looked pleadingly at him.

"No, go as far as you like. I like to talk about it too."

"I want to see everything in Paris—not just the Louvre and Versailles and the Tuileries. And not just the Bois de Boulogne and Montmartre and the restaurants, either. I want to see the part of Paris that's significant—where there are men and women who see clearly the

48

things that I've never been allowed to
see; where love and art and philosophy
are all a part of life; where gayety is
really gay and people dare to express the
big things that are in them. Do you
know what I mean, Bobby?"

"I guess so. You mean the Latin quarter, and all that, eh?"

Elizabeth was a little crestfallen. She
refused to have her exaltations pigeon-
holed.

"I suppose so—in a way. But what
I'm thinking of is in the air of Paris—it
must be! I can find the life I want any
where, I'm sure! And if I don't even—
there are so many other things. Father
can probably show me a lot. Did I ever
tell you about my father?"

"You've never seen him, have you?"

"Not since I was awfully little. But
I feel as if I know all about him, from
the things Mother is always so careful
not to tell me. He is wicked and disillusioned and a little enigmatic—a man
of the world." She caressed the phrase
with her tongue. "He's probably very

49

distinguished looking, with a cynical smile twisted on his lips and has seen and known and done everything. Life has nothing more to offer him. So he just stands by, looking on and laughing at the rest of us. He knows all there is to know about good food, good talk, good drinks. He is urbane and polished—and —and—cosmopolitan. He's everything that you, for instance, never will be, Bobby"—she smiled at him—her slow, superior smile.

Bobby grunted, but made no comment.

"That's my idea of romance," she went on vaguely. "Romance that comes of knowledge and disillusion and clear sight. Not back-porch romance, or innocent young love—or this sort of thing, either" — she indicated themselves, closely nestled in their nook. Bobby stirred uneasily.

"All this is so petty—so insignificant. It's an unskilled reproduction of something big and grand. It's a cheap imitation of passion—just as a lot of sentimental rubbish that we call love is really just a cheap imitation of love."

Bobby was interested, rather impressed. But he was also at this point unmistakably shivering, and considerably at a loss. He didn't know what to do or say. His own anticipation of Paris was quite different. It was made up of a jumble of anecdotes involving much delectable drunkenness, Zelli's, Kiley's, the Ritz Bar, certain restaurants, countless incomparable and amiably accessible little women. The latter presented something of a problem, the facing of which he had as yet side-stepped.

"Paris!" muttered Elizabeth, her curious throaty voice ringing a little. "Paris!"

Suddenly Bobby was startled to find his companion's two soft arms tightly about his neck, and to find her lips, warm and moist, throbbing passionately against his.

Fifteen minutes later they went inside.

51

CHAPTER 6.

The Inflection of the Monosyllable
Exhaustively Dealt With.

"THERE are," observed Mr. Willoughby
Quimby, gesturing expansively with a
very large cigar, "There are, nevertheless,
compensations in fatherhood."

"Yes?" said Mr. Frederick Fletcher,
comfortably applying fire to the end of a
similar cigar. Not a little of Freddy
Fletcher's position in life was directly
due to his manner of saying "Yes?"
There was doubt in it, a certain fine reserve. There was, moreover, assurance,
and an infinite understanding. It was
the most important thing he ever said,
and served him on almost all occasions
of note. An added value was given
"Yes" by Freddy's otherwise conspicuous taciturnity. He talked so very little

that it had even been wondered whether
he ever thought. Women, however, re-
ported, not without reticence, that he was
wont to become more voluble—on occasion. The occasions, unfortunately, had
this common quality: that there would
be no one present other than the lady addressed. So Freddy's reputation, soci-
ally, was almost wholly due to his talent
for intensive and sympathetic listening.
Every one liked to talk to Freddy—and,
on the whole, no one minded his own sar-
donic silences.

On this occasion, Mr. Quimby was
moved to enlarge on the more agreeable
phases of paternity.

"Here am I," said he, indicating himself gravely; "a man of middle age, without accomplishments, occupation, or resources. My educational background,
complete though it is, has unfortunately
become a bit obscured through the passing of years. My health may at any moment turn treacherous. The major
sweets of life, I think I may say, I have

tasted without reserve—certainly without scruple. And now where am I?"

"You are," murmured Freddy Fletcher with unexpected loquacity, casting an approving eye about the room, "in one of the most agreeable restaurants which it has pleased the masters of gastronomy to place at our disposal."

"There is the point!" exclaimed Mr. Quimby, no whit taken aback. "We have eaten well, drunk, I may say, deeply, are still drinking appreciatively"—he paused quite some time for a lingering sip of ancient brandy from a gigantic goblet. "But what of that? Montagné's is an accomplished fact. It offers no incentive to the sluggish ambition. We come here when we choose, we dine and wine, we pay our bill—that is"—(reproachfully) —"I pay our bill—and there's an end to it. The place has no secrets for us. There is never the joy of discovery—unless it be the rare one of a new dish. We have not the sense of adventuring on uncharted seas. We are only reliving again

and again our not very significant yes-
terdays."

"Humph!" remarked Freddy Fletcher.

"That's what I mean about being a
father!" proclaimed triumphantly Mr.
Quimby. His companion turned on him
a startled pair of black eyes.

"*What* do you mean?" he asked
sharply.

"Why, I mean just this: In my little
daughter I have a whole new universe
set before me. I see Paris and the world
about me freshly, through her eyes.
Think of it, man—think of me—old Willoughby Quimby—taking this charming
young person by the hand, going with
her to the Louvre, walking with her
through the by-ways of old Paris, show-
ing her parks, buildings, people! It will
be a new lease of life for me. I shall stop
drinking."

"Humph!" retorted Freddy Fletcher.

"I shall," went on Mr. Quimby, lyric-
ally, "turn over a new leaf. I, indeed,
have already done so,—and will, in a
sense, re-live my youth—Oh, how differ-

ently! Think of me, man—a father, a proud, respected, purified parent. When I hear her swift step on the stair—when I feel her slim arms about my neck, when we sit and read aloud to each other through the long evenings, think what it means to me!"

"I thought you said this embodiment of refreshing infancy had not yet arrived?"

"She hasn't. I anticipate," explained Willoughby Quimby.

"You do," agreed Freddy Fletcher, laconically.

They sat for a time in silence, bathing their appreciative souls in the fragrant smoke of their cigars and in the Napoleonic fumes of their brandy. The small room was about deserted. One party of transient Americans lingered at an adjacent table, talking a little more loudly than was strictly essential. A few waiters hurried about, doing whatever they were doing in adroit silence.

Freddy Fletcher, oddly, broke the pause. Said he:

"I have a feeling, Willoughby, that something unexpected is going to happen."

An agreeable maître d'hôtel, with the shoulders of a Firpo and the manner of a Chesterfield, was approaching their table.

"M. Quimby," he addressed that individual with the deference born of some years' largess; "your servant has just telephoned."

"What the devil does he want?"

"He beg me to tell M. Quimby that Mademoiselle his daughter has just arrived."

Mr. Quimby started violently, one hand tugging furiously at his hair.

"Good God! She can't have arrived. I can't have it! I have made other arrangements. My last night of freedom —and she assails it. She wasn't to arrive till tomorrow."

"I could say to M. Quimby's servant that M. Quimby has just left." The waiter was all solicitude.

"No." Mr. Quimby's face had resumed its calm. "No. I will go. My first impulse was unworthy of me. My dear little daughter!" And Mr. Quimby sighed heavily.

"Humph," continued Freddy Fletcher, abstractedly.

"And will you, Freddy, do me the great favor of calling up Tommy Sterling—Wagram 0203—and say that I shall perhaps be unable to attend the convivial assemblage which was to take place under his auspices this evening. Explain to him that I have just become a father."

"Uh-huh," assented Freddy, obligingly.

"And with that—I must be off to meet my child. When next you see me, my Frederick, I shall be no longer the flippant boulevardier. I shall be a family man—I shall no longer drink. Montmartre will no longer know me; Dan's will be without my enlivening custom. But years will have rolled off these tired shoulders of mine."

"Yes?" said Freddy Fletcher, as they rose to leave.

CHAPTER 7.

In Which Mr. Quimby Becomes a Father.

ARRIVED at his apartment house, situated vaguely near the Place de l'Étoile, Mr. Quimby went up in the elevator, pressed the button that sent it down again, and paused before a closed door. He felt decidedly ill at ease. He had, he felt, been denied an adequate period in which to adjust himself to the sudden changes in his status. He was in the mood of a man hesitating on the verge of a cold plunge or a bitter draught. Mr. Quimby disliked both bitter draughts and cold plunges. The easiest way had something very intimately to do with his philosophy of life. Abruptly the hardest way had come upon him.

At any rate, he was glad he had had a

good deal to drink. He was never at his best unless backed by the able coöperation of alcohol. In this instance, while far from drunk, he felt refreshingly able to deal adequately with almost any circumstance. A warm current of physical satisfaction flowed through his soft body. So he breathed deeply, fiddled thoughtfully with his key, finally rang the bell.

Joseph (more intimately, Joe) was a Frenchman of swarthy mien, moderate stature and prematurely gray hair. His face possessed the eloquent faculty of contorting itself into oddly expressive shapes and communicative wrinkles. When he opened his master's door, it was a study in acute perturbation. He took Mr. Quimby's hat and stick, however, without comment, and waited silently while the prospective parent adjusted the adjustable features of his attire before the mirror in the entrance hall. That process completed with some degree of care, Mr. Quimby addressed Joseph in a low tone.

"My daughter?"

"Mademoiselle is in the library. She is not alone, Monsieur."

"A gentleman is with her?"

"Both a gentleman and a lady, Monsieur."

"Hum!"

Mr. Quimby took another deep breath, thrust back his shoulders, thrust out his discreet little paunch, blinked his blue eyes, walked five steps, threw open a glass door with lace curtains, entered his library.

The large, oak-paneled room was indeed occupied by three persons. A very dark young woman reclined on a couch to the left smoking a cigarette. A somewhat less dark and apparently even younger woman sat in a leather easy chair, facing him diagonally to his right. A tall young man with tortoise-shell glasses smoked in front of the fireplace immediately in front of him. Mr. Quimby stopped and bowed in a rather courtly manner.

"Good evening. I have," said Mr. Quimby, "reason to believe that I am in

61

the presence of my beloved daughter.
Might I, without seeming unduly intru-
sive, inquire which of you ladies is she?
Under the circumstances, I feel called
upon to kiss some one, and it would smack
of incest for me to kiss my own offspring!
I, by the way, am Willoughby Quimby."

The lady on his left stirred a little and
knocked a cigarette ash over the back of
the couch on which she was stretched.
She was, it appeared, in evening dress,
and her arms were long and white. Her
face was white too, softly wrapped in a
great, low mass of black hair. Her lips
flamed like a dull ruby, and her eyes
rested on him in a dark calm under level
brows.

"Hullo, father. I'm Elizabeth."

Willoughby bowed again and his pale
blue eyes rested on her in thoughtful agitation. His daughter went on, in a curious throaty drawl:

"This is Lucille Grosvenor. She is
going to stay with us for awhile."

Willoughby Quimby bowed again,

gravely. Miss Grosvenor looked up at him with large, serious brown eyes.

"And your chaperone—the exemplary Miss So-and-So, of whom your mother wrote?" He again addressed his daughter.

"She is staying at the Mirabeau—if you know where that is. You can go and see her in the morning—early."

Willoughby Quimby shuddered.

"I'm sorry," he murmured, contritely. "I am, unfortunately, deplorably indolent. I can only see her in the morning —late."

His daughter laughed—a low, throaty laugh, not at all unpleasant.

"You're rather nice," she approved him, "but ever so different from the way I thought you'd be." She examined him critically. "You're not nearly so wicked-looking as I hoped—just a little dissolute."

He winced, advanced a few paces into the room, took a cigarette from a stand and lighted it. Then, very gently, he indicated the young man on the hearth.

"And this gentleman, my dear? He is not, I trust, a son who has escaped my memory?"

Elizabeth looked around in startled surprise.

"Oh," laughed Elizabeth, "I'd forgotten Bobby. Bobby—come show yourself. This is Bobby Duncan, father. He was on the boat coming over."

Mr. Quimby nodded amiably. Mr. Duncan mumbled something incoherent.

"You don't mind if Lucille stays with us a few days, do you, father?"—went on his daughter from the couch. He reflected that she had a beautiful body—a beautiful, luxurious body. "I thought she'd help soften the blow of a suddenly acquired parent, so I got her away from her family for awhile. And your funny man, Joe or whatever his name is, seemed to think you had room. As a matter of fact, Joe was suspiciously efficient about finding accommodations for unexpected ladies in what is supposedly the apartment of a man alone."

"Joe," remarked Mr. Quimby,

blandly, "is the acme of all that is resourceful."

Miss Grosvenor here spoke for the first time. Also she stood up and came pleadingly toward her host.

"Please, Mr. Quimby, don't let Elizabeth bully you into having me! I really could just as easily stay with my family, if it's the least bit inconvenient. You will be honest, won't you?"

Mr. Quimby was looking into the extraordinary pair of wide brown eyes. Mr. Quimby was partial to brown eyes. These were the kind in which you are said to lose yourself; large, open eyes, with nothing, no barrier, to keep you from going in—in—exploring the personality behind them. He examined the eyes critically, wondered about them; wondered, too, just why his interest should be so acutely aroused by so negligible a face. Meanwhile, he answered with difficulty.

"On the contrary, Miss Grosvenor, you'll be a god-send. You see I have only just had the distinction of making

65

my daughter's acquaintance, and you'll help us a lot in getting to know each other. The difficulty will be entirely on your side—and Elizabeth's. My place has always—my daughter's unworthy implication notwithstanding—been run from a purely male point of view."

The big brown eyes continued for some moments to cause Mr. Quimby acute discomfort. Then, suddenly, they brightened into another completely revealing smile and she held out her hand.

"Do you know, Mr. Quimby—I think you're too utterly beguiling for words! I think we'll like each other!" Mr. Quimby winced.

"Father," came Elizabeth's slow, deep voice. He turned with a little effort.

"Elizabeth," said Mr. Quimby, urbanely, "I'm a great believer in getting things straight in the first place. All lazy men are. It saves trouble later. So let me explain right now that I detest being called 'Father.' Besides, I'm not used to it, and my heart isn't all that it was.

66

Would it be awfully hard for you to call me by my first name?"

"It wouldn't, if you didn't have such an abominable first name. I might"—(doubtfully)—"call you 'Will.'"

"Do. You won't be the first, and I quite agree about 'Willoughby.'"

"Then—Will!"

"Yes, Elizabeth?"

"Do you mind if we go out tonight?"

"We? Tonight?"

"I mean Bobby and Lucille and I. You see—we have more or less planned to go on a party with a friend of Bobby's—another fellow. Montmartre and all that. You don't mind, do you? Of course, you could come along, if you like."

Mr. Quimby did not answer for a moment. Somehow, things weren't as he had expected. Yet he couldn't, for the life of him, say why. Things, after all, were exactly as he should have expected. The trouble was that he hadn't pictured his daughter as she was, at all. He had thought of her more like—well, like Lucille Grosvenor, then. His glance fell on that young person, sitting quietly in the great chair, big, eager eyes fixed on him. He turned away quickly. After all—what was the difference? Nevertheless, he was forced to admit, there was a difference.

What he really was disappointed in was, he realized, a perfectly selfish thing. He had thought of his daughter chiefly in relation to her effect on him. And he suddenly saw that she was going to act upon him in a totally different way. He missed in her the naïveté, the overwhelming simplicity which he had half-consciously anticipated. As far as his own life was concerned, he didn't see that the psychological result of association with her would affect it at all. Other things, though—he thought hesitantly—might. And again his eyes wandered toward Lucille. He did not think of his daughter's friend so much as a person. She seemed rather the embodiment of young simplicity. All of which had very little to do with the matter in hand. Of course, the children wanted to go out and see

68

Paris. All young Americans did, on arrival in the "modern Nineveh." He nodded cheerfully.

"Of course, I don't mind. But I can't go with you. As a matter of fact, I have a sort of an engagement myself." He couldn't, he thought, put himself in the position of being left at home while his daughter made merry. "How about this fourth party? Is he coming here?"

Here Mr. Bobby Duncan first made his presence noticeable. He stepped forward a pace and spoke, rather gruffly, with a militant assurance.

"No, sir," said he. "We're picking him up on the way."

"Ah," said Willoughby Quimby, smiling a little. "At the Ritz Bar, I take it?"

"How did you know that, sir?"

"Where in the world else would you find a young American on his first day in Paris?" rejoined Mr. Quimby, in surprise. The young man laughed uneasily.

"Afterwards, of course, you are going to Zelli's?"

"I suppose so."

"Well," good-humoredly went on Mr. Quimby, "I may see you there later. I don't know where I'm to be taken. In case not, I'll say good night now."

There was a period of movement and laughter, of the donning of cloaks and furs. Mr. Quimby escorted them to the head of the stairs.

"You'll find my car at the door. It's a Minerva. The mustache jutting out on the side is attached to the chauffeur. Tell him to come back for me when you get where you're going. Take care of yourselves and don't drink bad wine!"

Mr. Quimby re-entered his apartment, shut the door, gave Joe a few instructions. Then he walked back into the library and chuckled ironically. So this, he reflected, was fatherhood?

He went to the corner, poured himself a brandy and soda, and sat down before the fire. Joe busied himself about the room behind him.

"Joe!"

"Monsieur?"

"Don't forget that one of those ladies

is my daughter and the other her friend."

"Of course not, Monsieur!"

"Accordingly, don't be too proficient in their service. Don't for an instant overlook the fact that they are the *only* ladies whom you have ever served in this apartment."

"*Entendu,* Monsieur. I am discretion itself."

"Thank you, Joe. In a few minutes I am going out. If any one should call, I shall be at the Jardin de ma Soeur with Mr. Sterling."

CHAPTER 8.

Parental Responsibility Asserts Itself Ponderously.

MR. QUIMBY awoke next morning to a remote and at first unaccountable feeling of inquietude. The sensation was not usual with him and he paused to examine it. Physically, all appeared well. His head ached a little, and a pudgy hand on the counterpane twitched nervously—but these were not unaccustomed phenomena, and their cause easily assignable. Chiefly, he observed in himself an unwonted self-reproach. He puzzled over it, between sleeping and waking. It was years now since he had outgrown early morning repentance for the excesses of the night before. Besides—the events of the evening coming back to him piecemeal—he had, as he recalled it, been moderately temperate. He remembered meeting Tommy Sterling at the Jardin Club. He remembered going on to some place in Montmartre—Mitchell's, as a matter of fact. He remembered several bottles of wine. But he had, he was sure, retired in a relatively sober state.

Suddenly, in a flood of recollection, everything was clear. Last night paternity had crept, like a celestial visitation, upon him. There was the cause of this indefinable disquiet, this new sense of responsibility. That was why he should at this moment be up and about, instead of indolently nursing a hang-over in bed. Rolling quickly over, Mr. Quimby inspected his watch. Eleven-thirty. He swore softly, dropped his short legs over the side of the bed, rang for Joe. His excited impatience drove away all thought of luxurious delay. He plunged at once into the matutinal routine of shaving, bathing, dressing.

It was a refreshed and talcumed, albeit a trifle shaky, Mr. Quimby who opened the door to his sitting-room a half hour

73

thereafter. But he opened it in considerable trepidation. Joe had given him certain news of his daughter and her guest. He had learned, for example, that they had breakfasted at ten, risen immediately after, were presumably about the apartment. He felt in no condition to talk to strangers—particularly strange daughters.

Near the big French windows of the sitting-room, on a sort of cushioned chaise longue, sat a girl, reading. Her hair—a lot of it—was blurred about her head in a brown mist. Her dress was a soft, lustrous green in the sunlight. At his entrance, she looked up and smiled cheerfully. He saw the smile only dimly against the sunny background, but he felt its confiding friendliness.

"Good morning, Mr. Quimby! Isn't it adorable of you to be even lazier than we?"

For a moment Mr. Quimby was assailed by doubt. His memory in the first hours of his rising was always a bit clouded. Was this his daughter, or——?

74

With an effort—and, oddly, a feeling
akin to regret—he recalled that she
wasn't. His daughter had been the other
—the dark, thin girl. He ran his hand
nervously through his hair.

"Good morning. You cover me with
shame. Need I explain that I, too, tasted
of nocturnal wine?"

"Oh, did you? Where did you go?"
the eager voice took him up.

"Here and there. It isn't important.
You were at Zelli's?"

"Oh, yes! It was too wonderful for
words. I never had such a good time in
my life!" Lucille Grosvenor, Mr.
Quimby perceived, was given to the
superlative. On the other hand, he was
curiously not annoyed by her use of it.
He was conscious, somehow, of a mental
reservation behind the extravagant phrasing. The girl, he felt, did not lose her
own intellectual balance—however she
expressed herself. Her enthusiasms were
the result of an overpowering simplicity.
They were an outlet for exuberant youth,

never quite overstepping the bounds of careful judgment.

"I suppose you made the acquaintance of the incomparable Joe?"

"Joe?"

"Joe Zelli—'the original one.'"

"Oh, my, yes!" breathlessly. "He gave us the 'royal box' and called us all the things he was supposed to call us, and invited us to spend a week-end at his farm, and knew our names almost before we told them. And he was awfully discreet about not seeming to know you too well, when he found out Elizabeth was your daughter, and told us you were 'one of the best.'"

Mr. Quimby smiled.

"Do you know, it's almost a year since I've been to that place. I must go one of these days. It has personality. Funny thing, too. The room is repulsive, the wines are bad, the service is hopeless, the floor is too small, the attractions are unspeakable, the clientèle distasteful, the music only fair—and yet there's a fascination about it all, an atmosphere. It's

76

of course all due to Zelli himself. He has genius, that man. The greatest showman since Barnum. Men like him and Dan and Frank at the Ritz and George at the Crillon ought to go down in history —along with a few great cooks and maîtres d'hôtel."

"He *is* marvelous."

She had put down her book, and sat looking at him with the lucid brown eyes, calmly, interestedly.

"Where," he asked diffidently, "is my recently acquired daughter?"

"She just went out. Said she wanted to catch her first glimpse of Paris alone. She'll be back in about an hour, I think."

Mr. Quimby hesitated.

"Do you mind very much if I have breakfast here? It's not a complicated meal for me. You may find it a little unusual, but——"

"Why, of course not. Do go ahead and eat!"

Mr. Quimby smiled—a deprecating embarrassed smile.

"That is one of the peculiarities of my

77

breakfast. It isn't one of the kind you eat—exactly," he remarked. "There—I think I hear it coming."

Entered Joe, impassive, bearing on a tray a glass containing a thick, creamy beverage. Mr. Quimby took it, bowed to his guest, drank it almost at a gulp, put back the glass with his not quite steady hand.

"I think, Joe," said he, in French, "that we might repeat that."

Joe bowed and retired.

"What *is* it?" asked Lucille.

"A brandy flip," announced Mr. Quimby, apologetically. "Nourishing, invigorating, delectable. My day I find incomplete without one—or two."

Mr. Quimby, it will be perceived, had as yet contrived to delay consideration of the practical application of his decision to stop drinking. In any case, he might have argued, the form of his *petit déjeuner* was a thing not to be trifled with without injury to his constitution. After all, he would not be fanatical about his adoption of a temperate way of life.

Sitting in an easy-chair opposite Lucille Grosvenor, Mr. Quimby proceeded to light a cigarette—his first that day—and inhaling the blue smoke appreciatively, to inspect his companion with some interest. She still leaned back, her eyes resting on him, her hands clasped behind the mass of brown hair.

"Do you know," she began after a pause, "I think you're going to be very good for Betty."

"Why?" Mr. Quimby was startled. "I wouldn't be good for any one!"

"I think you'll handle her just as she needs to be handled."

"I think you're probably as completely wrong—if you'll permit me to think so—as you well could be. I know as little about how to handle a daughter as any man living. I'm utterly selfish, utterly self-sufficient. My habits are—not those of the model parent. My philosophy of life—such as it is—contains every idea that a young girl should be protected from. I am what is euphoniously known

79

as a *bon viveur*—only that and nothing more."

"That's exactly what I mean! Betty has already been much too carefully brought up. Mrs. Quimby is a wonderful woman——"

"Amen!" murmured Mr. Quimby, reminiscently.

"But I don't think she was quite what Betty needed. They never understood each other. And now Betty feels that she's free at last and can do all the things she's never been allowed to do and always wanted to. She's awfully likely to run completely wild."

"And you mean that I'm to restrain her?" Mr. Quimby's eyes were full of terror. He tugged frantically at his hair.

"No. That's just what I don't mean. Nothing could be worse than for you— or any one else—to try to 'restrain' Betty. She's broken loose and loose she'll stay."

"Then what am I to do?" helplessly pleaded Mr. Quimby.

"You are to let her strictly alone, to go her own way. She'll go it anyway—and in the long run it probably won't be a bad way." Mr. Quimby looked vastly relieved. "Meanwhile, though, she's very apt to get herself into all kinds of trouble. That's where *you* come in!"

Mr. Quimby groaned.

"What a place to come in!"

"You see——" Lucille leaned forward and began to explain energetically, wide-eyed and eager. "You see, Betty wants something and she doesn't at all know what. So blundering about looking for it, with any number of ideas and no experience and a sudden taste of freedom, she's bound to get herself into hot water —lots of times. Do you see what I mean?"

"I'm afraid so," lugubriously.

"Now—you can't keep her out of trouble. She's much too strong a personality. I'm her best friend and I know Betty better than any one else in the world knows her. So I'm sure I'm right about that. But you can get her out of it once she does get in—and before she gets in too far."

81

"What makes you think I can?"

"Because that's just the beauty of you."
Mr. Quimby inclined his head politely,
and took his second brandy flip from Joe.
"You see you're older and fairly wise.
You haven't any false sentiment and you
know all about things—I mean evil
things."

"You flatter me." She ignored him.

"You know exactly the sort of way a
girl like Betty is likely to get herself into
jams and you're just the sort of smooth,
unscrupulous, sophisticated person to
straighten things out before it's too late.
All you have to do is to keep an eye on
her and always be ready, in case anything
does happen. You must always be on
hand and know everything, without
seeming to interfere until you see something happening. And then do it with
tact."

Mr. Quimby finished his drink and lit
another cigarette in considerable perturbation. This matter of being responsible
for the happiness in life of another person was assuming alarming proportions.

"You don't mind my talking that way, do you, Mr. Quimby?" asked Lucille, in sudden alarm. "I know it isn't any of my business, but—but I do know Betty awfully well and I'm worried about her."

Mr. Quimby smiled genially.

"And I don't know her at all and I'm just about as worried. Meanwhile, I should say that my first job is to get acquainted with my precariously-situated daughter as quickly as possible. And I'll see what I can do about being all that you say I've got to be. But you'll have to help me."

"Of course! We'll make it an alliance for the salvation of Betty."

"Right! And—some time—you might just take enough time out to tell me a little about the girl. I at least have a right to start even!"

Willoughby Quimby was a bit panic-stricken. Things were coming to a head. He felt, however brave a front he might put up, hopelessly inadequate in face of the difficulties of his position. It was not a task that he could shirk. Why the devil hadn't Florence kept the girl home? he asked himself, angrily.

A ring at the door put a temporary end to Mr. Quimby's disturbed reflections.

CHAPTER 9.

Elizabeth Encounters a Great Adventure.

ELIZABETH QUIMBY went without delay
about the business of getting herself into
"trouble." Paris was, she felt at once,
all that she had expected it to be. She
thrilled responsively to every phase of
Gallic life. The theater pleased her;
the shops filled her with covetous joy, she
delighted to while away the afternoons
at boulevard cafés, rejoicing in a sense of
pleasurable, if wholly innocuous, liberty;
the restaurants outdid her fondest dreams
of epicurean indulgence; she followed
her father's dutiful paternity from museum to museum, to the Louvre and the
Luxembourg, to the Cluny and the
Musée Rodin, to the Trocadero and the
Invalides, to the Panthéon and Nôtre
Dame, to Sainte Chapelle and Sacré

Cœur, to the Salon and to that amazing
panoramic application of the science of
optics, the Panthéon de Guerre; she dined
with him—not infrequently accompanied
by Tommy Sterling, Freddy Fletcher,
or some other judiciously selected
acquaintance of his—at the Café de Paris
and Ciro's, in the Bois and along the
quais, at Voisin's and Montagné's, at
Foyot's and the Tour d'Argent, at Lapé-
rouse and Larue, at Paillard's and the
Marguéry, on the Place du Tertre and
at the Rendezvous des Mariniers, at
Francis' and the Trois Sergents de Ro-
chelle, at a dozen other esoteric corners
where Mr. Quimby, out of the fullness
of his gastronomic wisdom, felt that "one
eats well." They motored to Versailles
and Fontainebleau, to Chantilly, to Beau-
vais, even as far as Chartres. So the days
passed agreeably enough and Elizabeth
felt that she had at last reached a land
where she could fulfill her own expand-
ing destiny to its utmost capacity. Only
she remained a little vague as to the precise nature of that destiny.

Paris she approved whole-heartedly. Parisians she accepted with reservations. Her father she found an agreeable companion, a polished and accomplished host, a model of suave tact. She was a little disappointed in his character. His much-anticipated wickedness was at most an inconspicuous adjunct to his nature as she saw it. She regretted that he could not be led, if not off his carefully maintained good-behavior, at least to talk of his prior misconduct. But there was a certain fascination in the reflection that below the exemplary exterior lay one knew not what depth of occult infamy.

On most of their expeditions, Elizabeth and her father were accompanied by Lucille Grosvenor, now living with her own parents, but constant companion of the Quimbys. Elizabeth was gratified to find her friend expansively accepted by the father on whom she herself had been so unceremoniously thrust. Mr. Quimby's generous parenthood seemed to spread itself over each of them with equal consideration. At times his hospitality was almost too eager for Elizabeth's taste. She was a little irked by Lucille these days. She felt something almost hostile in the other girl's quiet enthusiasm. Lucille was naïvely interested in everything, always ready with a wide-eyed superlative of praise or condemnation. But she lacked the heroic unrest that was at the bottom of Elizabeth's enthusiasms. She had an unsatisfactory way of being contented with things as they were, whereas Elizabeth took nothing at its face value, regarded everything as only a manifestation of something great and eternal which in some obscure way had a lot to do with Elizabeth's own dreams and anticipations.

For all of Elizabeth Quimby's deep draughts of the enchanted atmosphere of the holy city, she had not yet met her great adventure. She felt its skirts brush past her in the damp night air; saw its shadow in the mist over the Seine; heard its footfall in the winding streets of old Paris. But she had not yet encountered it face to face; did not, in fact, have much idea of what form it would elect to take.

She felt, somehow, that it had a good deal to do with love—presumably because Elizabeth was a woman and very fond of her rich, beautiful body. Presumably, also, it was because Elizabeth was a girl of acute sensibility and because she lived almost wholly for her senses. She had her father's love of food and drink and luxury. Beauty, in art, in the human form, in drama, caught at her heart, leaving her a little breathless. And she was eminently, feverishly, theatrically, sex-conscious.

So, shorn of their serio-comic grandiloquence, Elizabeth's aspirations were not particularly complex. All she wanted, quite simply, was a man. Not just any man—but a man who could embody for her all the large secret dreams of her adolescence. He must have enough of the unfathomable, enough of mystery, to represent for her the whole of the great mystery of sex. Freedom, the freedom of which Elizabeth talked and thought so much, meant actually freedom to love and be loved, on the grand, exalted scale to which her not quite morbid imagination had elevated love.

All of which being the case, it was not particularly extraordinary that Elizabeth intuitively saw the beginning of her great adventure in the significant black eyes of Conway Cross. For it was an avocation with Conway Cross to gratify just such obscure longings in the women of his acquaintance. He was well known to the habitués of Dan's—a tall, boldly handsome gentleman of a not unusual type, with polished black hair and an unscrupulously aquiline nose. A born lover, this Conway Cross, and he had not let his talents rust. His suave tongue, his expressive eyebrows, his elaborate studio, his position of patrician dilettante in the realm of art (he was not lacking in a crafty kind of deftness with the brush), all helped him in the career which made him the envied hero of many a whispered tale along Dan's brass rail.

Willoughby Quimby presented him

quite casually to his daughter. But Willoughby Quimby did not see Cross's adept gaze search his daughter's, holding her unwary glance until he had drawn from it the answering flicker of an incipient understanding. Their meeting then had been brief and commonplace, but Conway Cross's sure instinct made him scent a possible sequel. And Elizabeth, her heart responding tumultuously to his judiciously chosen phrases of polite greeting, suddenly saw the great adventure bowing before her.

Which would have been all very well and all very unimportant if capricious destiny had not led Elizabeth one bright June morning, just at luncheon time, along the Rue Boissy d'Anglas at the precise moment when Conway Cross, on his way to keep an appointment at the Crillon, was walking along that same street. The upshot of this meeting, Elizabeth's state of mind being what it was and Conway Cross being who he was, was predictable. A quarter of an hour later found them both in Cross's famous studio, located extravagantly near the Champs Élysées, while the painter himself telephoned the tidings of sudden indisposition to the Crillon, his servant busied himself resignedly about an unforeseen *déjeuner à deux* and Elizabeth dabbed agitatedly at her nose with a powder puff. The great adventure began to seem disconcertingly imminent.

It was not until Conway Cross, with some pride and considerable aptness of phrase, had displayed to her the intensely hued and adroitly painted pictures of his making, and the meal—served on a broad stone balcony overhanging the garden of an adjoining hotel—was well under way, that their conversation shifted from the sparkling commonplaces he dispensed so well to a field in which he was even more versed.

"You are," said Conway Cross, applying butter with extravagant liberality to a thin slice of toast, "extraordinarily beautiful." He put a great deal of the slice of toast in his mouth and munched placidly.

"So I am reliably informed." Elizabeth took the precaution of a liberal sip of claret.

Conway Cross swallowed his toast and resumed.

"You are, further, not at all unintelligent."

"And you, if I may say so, are pleasantly discerning."

"You have probably," went on her host, waving his knife expressively, "never been adequately loved."

"For that, you can hardly scold me. If that is so, I can assure you it is positively not my fault."

"When I call you beautiful," reverted Conway Cross, "I do not, if you'll allow me to make the reservation, refer to your face—admirable face though it is."

"My face," said Elizabeth sadly, "is one of the things that are much better unreferred to."

"Nor do I imply any superlative spiritual, mental, or moral pulchritude. I do not deny its existence—I merely refrain from affirming it."

"You have the sweetest way of dissembling your compliments," drily observed Elizabeth Quimby. "Would it be too much—or indelicate—for me to ask you bluntly in what respect you *do* find me beautiful?"

Conway Cross's pointed gaze held hers unwaveringly for a moment.

"You have," he remarked, without emphasis, "one of the most beautiful bodies it has ever been my good fortune to look upon. You have the body of an evil saint; a body made first of all for passion, lust, for the eternal, triumphant desires of men, yet a body cut in the hardest and chillest alabaster; a body, even, that would be not unworthy a niche in some cloud-formed temple, where it might float like the wraith of eternal loveliness to torment the searching heart of man. So it is for the warm, sculptured flesh of you, brutally and wonderfully and shamelessly, that I think I am beginning to love you, Elizabeth Quimby."

She sat very still and white and a little frightened then, with a queer thrilling

94

pain under her breasts and a forkful of succulent *broccoli* poised over her plate. A cool little wind ran over the green lawn below them, leaped to their balcony, stirred the lace doilies on the table.

Elizabeth was looking out over the garden and she was vaguely conscious that it was a charming garden. There were beds of flowers along the four walls —lavender and yellow and rose, come newly from brown earth to test the sufferance of young Spring. A graveled path made a white rectangle between the flowers and the lawn in the middle and a little marble faun stood in a fountain on the lawn, the water running pleasantly off his round, vigorous shoulders, down his smooth back and thighs. The fountain hung about him in a veil of silver and sun-gold, and embedded in its soft mist was a glowing arc of refracted color. The grass was a solid caressing green, and the sunlight over it and the flowers and the fountain had color and texture, so that those two on the balcony were cloaked in a warmth of lucent gold.

Then Elizabeth Quimby raised her fork to her lips and smiled a little unsteady smile.

"Don't you think, Mr. Cross," said she, "that your observations are based on rather inadequate investigation? It's not awfully flattering that you single out those particularly of my charms which are rather intimately screened from inspection of the inquiring male."

"An intuition of form," he replied academically—"notably of the human form—is at least a part of my métier. And when my instinct for physical excellence is whetted by my response to your bewitching individuality, no material barriers can be any considerable obstacle to my percipience."

She laughed.

"It's unfair of you to bludgeon my seemly diffidence with the sheer weight of vocabulary. I feel as if you had verbally undressed me."

"Which is no reason at all why you shouldn't finish the meal I have caused to be set before you. My approbation of your anatomy is no excuse for neglect of its nutrition."

Whereupon Elizabeth tractably resumed eating and Conway Cross continued talking, steering the conversation deftly from art to climate, from the current theater to current scandal, from life to love.

Meanwhile the moist marble faun in the garden disported himself in his fountain, and shadows began to drag their long shapes across the grass and up the walls. Dessert—a complicated sweet—came and went, coffee and richly-tinted liqueurs were poured from geometrically shaped decanters, cigarettes were placed before them—fat, oriental cigarettes. Over the balcony balustrade floated the blue smoke, mingling in a scattering haze with the sunlight. From far away came the high squeak of auto horns, the mirthful hum of a Paris afternoon, the shrill voice of a woman crying papers.

Elizabeth felt warm and comfortable, her veins alive with a calm happiness. She was able, she felt, to lay her mind in the hands of this man who would examine it, comprehend it, caress it. She felt a confident satisfaction in their enclosed proximity, with the world she had always known shut out beyond the golden veil of sunlight. She felt free and curiously secure. It pleased her to listen to her companion's quiet, cadenced voice, to feel the thrill of his swift plunges into a bold intimacy and of the equal celerity of his timely withdrawals to the entertainingly commonplace. She felt the electric stimulus of the *Grand Marnier*.

As to Conway Cross, there was nothing actually insincere in his attitude toward Elizabeth or any other woman. That was perhaps a part of the artistic impulse in him. He treated a woman as a canvas to be covered, as an instrument to be played. His interest was held as long as the instrument responded. A firm rebuff cooled his ardor instantly. So did complete triumph. His interest was wholly in the process of seduction. Once there was no more to attain, he would relinquish the attainment, with hardly a backward thought. He was not, primarily, a voluptuary. He was predatory—but he was much more the sportsman than the hunter. He delighted in the chase for its own sake, in the kill only as the symbol of success. He was wholly selfish, of course, in a naïve, boyish way. His cruelties (and all his amours ended cruelly; infamously, if you will) troubled him vaguely, but he could no more have helped them than he could have altered his own not very complex personality. Fundamentally he was a child, playing with toys, building houses of blocks only to destroy them on their completion. Or, he was an artist, creating out of the fierce inner necessity which compels the artist to create, without in any wise compelling him to cherish the creation.

Later, they went inside and Conway Cross showed her about the studio. His own work stood on easels, leaned against the wall, cluttered the floor in confused heaps. Exotic canvases, most of them: odalisques, with great curving thighs,

99

reminiscent remotely of Matisse; garish
dancing girls; intimate interior groups;
a few compositions frankly porno-
graphic. He talked on one theme or another, seizing picture or object as a start-
ing point for any divergence of a fertile
if not particularly fundamental intelligence.

They sat on a divan in the corner—one
of those divans piled with cushions and
bright fabrics in judicious disarray.
Conway Cross, alert to seize the mood of
the moment, was silent. So for a long
time there was very little sound, and they
smoked together, so aware of each other's
presence and of its significance that the
mutual consciousness because almost a
barrier between them.

Elizabeth, languid among the cushions, felt her heart beating faster. Her
nails dug into her palms. Suddenly she
was beginning to feel the hot urge of her
sex. Anything would have been a relief.
If he had kissed her, taken her hand—it
would have broken the link of desire that

connected them. Suddenly she rose, and looked at him.

"I suppose I must go. My father will be waiting."

Conway Cross got up slowly.

"I don't think you should go," he said. She was silent, looking at him.

"We have made of this," he said quietly, "a meeting not unlike others. But there has come between us a little flame, feeding on the fuel of our understanding. Something warm and sudden and incomparable has grown up in the fusion of our personalities. It is in our power to complete it or to shatter it.

"You are not like the woman they have made of you. In your emotions you are a soaring, free thing, capable of flights that your habit of thought cannot permit you to conceive. None of us are allowed to touch infinity more than a few times. I think"—he looked at her steadily and eagerly—"I think we are both on the point of touching it, now, together.

"Are you going?" said Conway Cross, after a pause.

Elizabeth gave him a helpless, ago-nized look—fearing the cup he had put to her lips. When he took her in his arms she yielded with a little moan.

CHAPTER 10.

Mr. Freddy Fletcher is Loquacious.

MR. QUIMBY walked disconsolately into Dan's and ordered an orangeade. Dan, with a slight frown of displeasure, relegated the construction of the drink to an assistant.

It was ten o'clock one evening about a week following the episode in Conway Cross's studio. Elizabeth and Lucille Grosvenor were dining with Bobby Duncan and some of that young man's friends. Mr. Quimby was flung wholly on his own resources.

Dan was sympathetic, but a little distant. He was a kindly man and tolerant, but it was inevitable that he should be a shade less cordial to Mr. Quimby not drinking than to Mr. Quimby drinking.

The orangeade diminished slowly.

Mr. Quimby's enthusiasm for it waned. He longed to take one real drink—only one to restore his self-respect. That he dared not to do so hurt the self-respect more than anything else. But the fact remained that on the three preceding days Mr. Quimby had taken one drink— only one—and by some inexplicable means that one drink had multiplied and propagated until the furthest flight of Mr. Quimby's fancy could not persuade him that he was a strictly sober man. If you took one drink, you might as well take two—even three; if you took three, a fourth scarcely altered your status; and somewhere shortly after the fifth or sixth came that nebulous dividing line beyond which there was no end to the succession of your refreshment. So, at least, Mr. Quimby had found, not alone this week but in the course of a long career, much of it devoted to the experimental study of intoxicants. So, at last, facing the situation with a resigned frankness, he had been compelled to proscribe even that first. His worst agony lay not in a consuming thirst, not even in the social discrepancy attendant upon abstinence. It lay in an overwhelming *ennui*. The world and its inhabitants ceased to hold any interest for Mr. Quimby. His tongue had lost its fluency; his eyes were without luster; the hours dragged wearily.

On this occasion, the monotony was varied by the timely entrance of Freddy Fletcher, who nodded gravely to Mr. Quimby, and ordered a *fine* from Dan.

"I haven't had a drink today," announced Mr. Quimby, gloomily.

Freddy Fletcher eyed the orangeade with frank distaste.

"I think you're a fool," he remarked, categorically.

Mr. Quimby acquiesced humbly, carried the orangeade to a table, sat down heavily. Freddy Fletcher followed him.

"Why aren't you drinking?"

"My daughter——" began Willoughby Quimby, wearily.

"Rot! I've known your daughter about as long as you have. She doesn't give a whoop whether you're drunk or sober."

"She doesn't care, I know. But I can't very well be an adequate parent when I'm full of liquor."

Freddy Fletcher conceded the point reluctantly. But he looked sharply over at his companion and lit a cigarette.

"Perhaps you're right. What I really mean is that whether that has anything to do with it or not, your chief reason for clambering on the mineral chariot is something else."

Mr. Quimby's pale eyes turned on him in frightened inquiry.

"Meaning——?"

"That you're rapidly trying to make a fool of your respected, if somewhat portly, self."

"I don't understand."

"You ought to. How old are you, Will?"

"Less than half a century."

"You look at least fifty-five. How old is Lucille Grosvenor?"

Mr. Quimby looked around in alarm.

The young American, Ward Johnson, was the only other person in the room. He was standing out of ear-shot, at the bar, rolling dice with Dan for his next five drinks.

"What difference does it make? Do you mean to imply that I——? She's about nineteen."

"It won't do, Will. It won't do."

"Don't be absurd, Freddy! I'm not a fool, if I do look it. Lucille is a friend of my daughter's. So am I. Thus we are occasionally thrown together. I am trying to be a father to both of them."

"A father?"

"A father. Probably the only possible relationship between man and woman with which I have never before familiarized myself is that between father and daughter. I find the experience salutary and refreshing."

"Yes?" commented Freddy Fletcher, as though, having said his say, he was prepared to close the discussion. Mr. Quimby, however, was not quite finished. He continued in some agitation.

"That's the trouble with this life, here. You people can't see past your own drooling noses. Anything clean and wholesome is quite beyond your comprehension. Why can't I see a good deal of a girl half my age—less than half—a friend of my own daughter, without your filthy implications?"

"I'm not implying anything filthy," mildly remonstrated Freddy Fletcher. "On the contrary, I am implying that into the objectionable muck of your extremely agreeable but somewhat disorderly life has come something young and fragile and rather lovely. I imply that for the first time since you were old enough to sneer at youth, you, Mr. Willoughby Quimby, have permitted your worldly-wise old self to fall naïvely and boyishly in love. And my heart goes out to you because it is such a grand and pathetic and futile sort of thing to do."

"But——"

"Wait a minute. In spite of all that I can't help telling you that you'd better take immediate steps to alter your state of mind, or you're likely to contrive a good deal of unhappiness for you and the girl both."

Mr. Quimby drank some of his orangeade and ran his hand uneasily through his hair.

"Put it that you're right—and I don't for a minute admit it—why shouldn't I love the child? Why shouldn't I ask her to marry me, for instance?"

"In the first place, because she'd refuse you and you'd put yourself into an absurdly humiliating position. Don't forget, Will, that you aren't the man you were fifteen years ago, when, I understand, women contrived to extract amorous pleasure from the very gleam of your hair. Now you haven't even got all the hair left. You're stout, you're a drunkard. In the next place, if she accepted you for any reason—well, you know yourself how happy either of you'd be a year later. Why don't you forget it while there's still plenty of time? You aren't an old man yet, Will, but you're old enough to make an unholy ass out of your-self."

"Has any one else got this absurd no-tion about us?" sharply asked Mr. Quim-by. Freddy Fletcher shook his head.

"No. I don't suppose any one will," said he, simply. He was not at all un-aware that his perceptions of human re-lationship were keener than most peo-ple's. And he was proud of the fact that his friends had always been able to rely on his discretion. Mr. Quimby, for ex-ample, did not even think it necessary to ask him to keep his suspicions to himself.

Freddy Fletcher sipped his brandy thoughtfully for awhile.

"By the way," he remarked finally, his eyes fixed on his glass; "I saw Eliza-beth this afternoon at Armenonville with Conway Cross."

Mr. Quimby looked up quickly.

"Sure?"

"Sure."

"Hum. She told me she was going shopping."

"Probably met him on the street."

"She has met him on the street altogether too often lately, damn the fellow. I hope he isn't annoying her."

"She didn't look annoyed, this afternoon."

"Another of your insinuations?"

"No. But I don't think Conway Cross is good company for any girl. Do you?"

"Elizabeth can take care of herself. I've told her what kind he is."

"Just the same——"

"Damn it, Freddy, I can't keep the girl on a leash! Seeing Cross will probably teach her a few things—do her good."

"Teach her a few things she might better learn from some one else."

"She'll send him away if he bothers her."

"And if he doesn't bother her?"

"Anyway, Cross is no worse than others. Only cruder. He's no worse than—than I am, if you come down to that."

"Handsomer," commented Freddy Fletcher, laconically.

"He knows better than to try any of his stuff on Elizabeth."

"Does he?"

"If he doesn't, she'll soon show him. I know Elizabeth."

"Do you?"

"Do you think you know her better?" belligerently.

Freddy Fletcher was silent.

"I might just as well keep her from seeing you," resumed Mr. Quimby. "You drink a good bit yourself, you haven't a particularly clean record with women, and you aren't bad looking. How old are *you*?"

"Thirty-four. At least I have a few shreds of decency. Conway Cross hasn't."

"Granted. But the whole thing's absurd. She hardly knows him."

"I'm taking Elizabeth to lunch tomorrow," mused Freddy Fletcher.

"You might see what your influence will do," ironically suggested Willoughby Quimby.

"I might."

"Don't forget you're dining with us

Wednesday. You'll have a chance then to take back everything you've said to-night."

"Yes?" said Freddy Fletcher, thoughtfully.

Willoughby Quimby rose suddenly.

"Damn it," said he "I can't stay in here any longer. Dan may put me out any minute anyway. Coming my way?"

"Meeting Tommy Sterling here in a few minutes. Want to come on a party?"

"Are you trying to torture me? I'm not drinking."

"You will be."

"Want to bet?"

"Never on a sure thing. Good night."

"Good night. Good night, Dan."

Freddy Fletcher watched Mr. Quimby's receding back through the door. Then he sighed and ordered another *fine*. He had not talked so much in weeks, and he could not see that his talking had done much good. Futile thing, talk. He had been a fool to indulge in it, he concluded. Still—he was worried.

CHAPTER 11.

Mr. Quimby Observes Himself Dispassionately.

ARRIVED at his rooms, Mr. Quimby sank sadly into an easy chair. In all his varied experience of the world he had never, until now, adequately perceived what a wholly depressing place it was. A drink or two, now, would put a different face on things. He looked wistfully over at the brandy decanter in the corner.

Curious, that notion of Freddy Fletcher's about him and Lucille. He wondered just how much truth there was in it. More, certainly, than it was pleasant to admit. There was that quickening of his heart-beat when she came into the room. There was the thrill at her nearness, the warm satisfaction at even the thought of her. He laughed bitterly to himself. He ought to have outgrown that sort of thing. At his age—with his experience—mooning like a schoolboy. And, after all, what did it amount to? It simply meant that her freshness and simplicity had come into his life as a novelty, a new sensation. He was getting from her exactly what he had looked forward to from his daughter. But what had he to do with freshness and simplicity? Beastly bore, at best. Drive him crazy after a while. Already, in spite of his feeling for her, he could not help an occasional shiver of distaste at her perpetual superlatives. In his world, the superlative had no existence—save as a comic medium.

Certainly he had no idea of marrying the girl. The most he could hope for was a cheerful few weeks' companionship—a new and salutary sensation, which might entail some rather fundamental alterations in his own jaded point of view. She would never know his feeling. It would be an outrage to soil the clean youth of her with his shop-worn, middle-aged tenderness. Meanwhile, he could do his best to straighten out his own life, to try to get back as nearly as he could to the ideals of youth. He was not particularly sentimental or theatrical about it. There was, he honestly felt, nothing wrong with his life as he had lived it. But, at the same time, he flattered himself that he had never been in any rut. He was a flexible enough personality to be the other thing, too. The fact that he had been a middle-aged *roué* was no reason why he should not plunge boldly into the fountain of youth and regale himself for a while with a less trammeled emotional experience.

Meanwhile, there was nothing he wanted quite so much as a drink. How else spend the evening? He could go to bed—but it would be hours before he could sleep. He was not used to sleeping as early as this or when he lacked the soporific reaction from alcohol. Also, he was remotely and indefinably worried. He could read—but his attention wandered from the book. He was not much of a reader. He could write letters, but the very thought revolted him.

Over at Dan's he could find friends. At any café he could find cheer. Montmartre in an hour would be a blaze of light and merriment. Mr. Quimby sighed and went out for a walk. He walked for an hour, sat at a café *terrasse,* drank a *citron pressé.* Full of fruit juices, now, he went home again, fidgeted around the room. He undressed, took a warm bath. Then he went to bed, quivering with nervous irritation. All night he thrashed about the bed, crumpling the sheets, tossing off the blankets. At about six o'clock he fell fitfully asleep.

CHAPTER 12.

La Vie de Bohême.

THERE was at that time a restaurant and pseudo-American bar known as the Café des Fous, located on the heights of Montparnasse. It was less than a block distant from those twin purveyors of bohemianism to the curious, the Dôme and the Rotonde. It was not appreciably different from a number of similar places which have had their fleeting vogue in "the quarter" and gone their eventual way into a pleasing obscurity.

The Café des Fous was conscientious about the implications of its name. King Madness reigned there in all his least agreeable aspects. The café's clientèle was chiefly Anglo-American. Its prices were not immoderate. Its success was dependent on the discriminating extension of credit. As credit could not discriminatingly be extended to its out-at-elbows clients, it was only a question of time before its *patron,* his confidence in humanity destroyed, would see fit to frown upon even the most plausible plea for delayed payment, and the tattered, inebriate throng who were its habitués would betake themselves to the more tolerant of his competitors. The *patron* himself was a bewildered, unhappy-looking Frenchman with a carefully-trimmed imperial, who (ungifted in tongues) conversed with his guests through the intercession of a beefy French-Canadian bartender, whose French was not worse than his English, whose cocktails were sublimest horror to the palates of the discriminating, whose qualifications for his post consisted in an elastic grin and an admirable capacity for sustained intoxication.

It was to this sanctum of expatriate indigence that Conway Cross one day conducted Elizabeth Quimby, in the course of a carefully plotted excursion to those

parts of Paris which her father had seen
fit to omit from his own educational itin-
erary. Those two had met often since
the momentous luncheon in his studio—
surreptitious meetings, all of them, for it
was felt that Mr. Quimby's approbation
of intimacy between Cross and Elizabeth
was not to be counted on. So, escaping
on one excuse or another from the pa-
rental fold, Elizabeth was wont to slip
hurriedly to a secluded rendezvous and
spend an exciting hour or so with her
lover, not infrequently ending in a subsequent discreetly contrived hour or so
in the studio. When seen together by her
father or his friends, Elizabeth could
quite simply mention a "chance meeting." So Conway Cross's intrigue pros-
pered. So Elizabeth's "great adventure"
grew greater and greater.

The Café des Fous was always crowded
at eight o'clock in the evening. This
evening was no exception. Elizabeth
and her escort were greeted by a reek of
onions and alcohol. The little bar was
packed with noisy, sweating, cheerful

folk, clamoring for drinks and more drinks. The *patron* sat behind it, his mustaches bristling in agitation, his plump cheeks quivering, his scared eyes roaming wonderingly over the flushed faces before him. The beefy bartender grinned and dropped his cocktail shaker, made mistakes, spilled gin, poured himself another drink. An enveloping mass of a woman with a round, good-natured face and a not inadequate voice sang an obscene song. The crowd joined in a roaring, discordant chorus.

Cross led his companion to a table in the rear of the place and a harassed waiter took their order—hors d'œuvres, a *tournedos,* a pint of claret.

"Probably," remarked Conway Cross, "if you asked every one of those people separately what they thought of this place, their answers would be identical."

"All of them enthusiastic?"

"All of them would inform you with eloquence that they hate the Café des Fous; that the life of the quarter is wholly demoralizing, fatal to any sort of

work, to health, to morale; that they
themselves don't belong here and only
come from time to time as 'onlookers,'
because it amuses them. You may come
here night after night for months and
ask the same question—they will always
be here—their answer will always be the
same. They will all explain solemnly
that they belong—really—on the other
bank. That is, if you get them alone in
a corner. Their ostensible pose is, of
course, carefree, artistic poverty."

"Aren't any of them sincere?"

"Sincere? They all are. But they all
know the truth about the quarter. They
all know that it is a slimy monster with
a strangle hold on them. Feebly, they're
still struggling, and their struggle takes
the form of a romantic assumption that
the peril doesn't exist. On the other
hand, they have no false pride. Not one
of them is at all reticent about the fact
that he is dead broke, that he gets drunk
every night, that he would be glad to
have you pay for his drink or his dinner,
that he would be even more delighted

to borrow some money from you. Those things are corner-stones of Anglo-Saxon Bohemia in Paris."

Conway Cross paused to greet friends in the gathering. The stout lady who had been singing pounced upon him to plant a fat, affable kiss on his mustache; a brief colloquy reëstablished her at the bar with a drink before her at Cross's expense. A lean, leathery individual with a wide, shrewd grin joined them long enough to borrow twenty francs. A chronically dirty looking gentleman sat down and began to explain crapulously his recent triumphs in the field of art. A ten franc loan removed him.

Cross pointed out a few celebrities. There was Huntington Dodge, a painter and illustrator with an international reputation. There was Paul Fisher, the newspaper man. There was Ethel Rainders, whose recent divorce had been a sensation. There was Ian MacGregor, scion of one of the noblest families in all England.

"What are they doing here? Sight-
seeing?" asked Elizabeth.

"No. They come because they like it.
The place, for some obscure reason, has
a fascination. Every one in Paris, rich
or poor, famous or infamous, drunk or
sober, turns up here sooner or later.
There is always romance in the idea of
Bohemia, if not in the fact. And I have
a feeling that the fact has never, Murger
to the contrary notwithstanding, been
much more lovely than the Café des
Fous. It's all in the point of view.
Granted the seeing eye, there's as much
romance and drama right here as there
ever was on the 'Boul Mich' in the palmy
days we have been taught to sigh for.
After all, poverty and carelessness and
dirt and genius ignored are about the
same the world over. I like the Café
des Fous—in small doses."

They ate in silence for a while, Elizabeth pleasantly excited. This was, after
all, a phase of life she had never before
known. Life, too, stripped to its most
blatant essentials. She found the conver-

sation about her stimulatingly coarse.
Humanity, in the Café des Fous, was de-
prived of its last privacies. The primary
natural functions of man entered quite
casually into the table talk of their neigh-
bors, and if a spade was consistently referred to by an opprobrious epithet, the
effect was less horrifying than thrilling
to Elizabeth's hitherto sheltered ears.

When their coffee arrived in shimmer-
ing little percolators, Conway Cross
looked closely at Elizabeth and spoke
softly.

"Have you decided?" he asked.

"Decided what?" she looked at him
with wide, startled eyes.

"Decided to give yourself—for a
while—wholly to love. Decided to leave
all this muck and take the beauty which
we have nurtured to where it can bloom
unsullied."

"I asked you not again to refer to that,"
said Elizabeth, quietly.

"How can you ask me not to refer to
what has become the pivot of my existence? It is as though I stood at the gates

of Paradise and Peter asked me not to
refer to the possibility of my admission.
It is as though I were starving, entered a
restaurant, began to order a meal, and
the waiter coldly asked me not to refer
to food."

Elizabeth laughed — her gentle,
throaty laugh.

"You ask too much—or not enough.
You ask me to tear up my life for the
sake of a week of poetry."

"Is not a week of poetry worth ten
lives?" explosively demanded Conway
Cross.

"Haven't we enough poetry here?"
asked Elizabeth, almost querulously.
"What more can you ask? I have given
you myself—body and soul; and still you
want more."

"What is it to possess you here? To
snatch at sordid secret moments, when I
might own you wholly? And I do not
ask much—only a few days, a week, of
Arcady. Our love is too delicate to stifle
in this way. We have made too much
beauty to have to hide it like a nursemaid

hiding her amour with the butler. We have at last caught sight of the summit of delight. Are we to turn back?"

"And after your week of Arcady—?"
He shrugged his shoulders.

"Who shall say? The future is in the lap of the gods. Only we have it in our power to create an ecstacy such as no one has known since time began, and we are turning the gold of it to trash. Come with me, Elizabeth! Come—so that I may show you what it is to be loved in the delicious present, leaving the future to the empty dreams of fools."

"Where would we go?"

"Anywhere. Away from everywhere, to where we could be alone with our own souls. No one need ever know."

"What could I tell my father?"

"That you were going motoring with friends—visiting—anything. Even he need not know."

"Do you think that would be any less a falsehood than to continue as we are?"

"Of course. Once out of Paris and we are free—free to give ourselves to the infinity of a perfect union. Here we are like children playing an obscene game. Elsewhere we would be divinities, knowing reality. And possessing reality in each other. I want you, Elizabeth; I want to possess you, utterly."

"It occurs to me," Elizabeth's voice came in her throaty drawl, "that your avowal would be almost as moving if couched in the more conventional form of a proposal of marriage."

Conway Cross did not move, but his eyes held a hurt look, as though she had put a dagger to his breast.

"Marriage," he repeated, tonelessly, "Marriage."

Then his voice grew somber.

"I had not thought you would say that. I thought you were above that. I thought, at last, that I had found one to whom love was a mad fusion of two souls—not the commercial union of two interests. Did you mean that? Because, if so, we must part."

Elizabeth accepted the rebuke meekly.

"You know I didn't. The remark was in bad taste."

"It was immoral," continued Cross reproachfully. "And, in any case, absurd. The idea is profanation of a feeling like ours. You believe in my devotion?"

"May I believe in it?"

"You must believe in it. We are one, we two, come together in the hands of a sublime destiny. Shall we not make our oneness whole? Come away with me, Elizabeth—now, tonight."

She was still for a moment, her eyes staring deeply across the room. Slowly she shook her head.

"No," murmured Elizabeth, sadly.

A fierce clamor of voices, a well-chosen oath or two, came from the bar. The lean, intelligent-looking man who had spoken to Cross was engaged in a resolute endeavor to pummel the face of a tow-headed youth who in his turn had clutched his assailant's throat in two chubby fists. They rocked back and forth across the room, glasses were knocked from a table, the table went over, the *patron* babbled excitedly, the bartender grinned, the rest of the crowd cheered. Came a splintering crash as the combatants blundered through the glass door onto the sidewalk. A noise of tongues. Conway Cross quickly rose, took Elizabeth by the arm, led her out another door.

"Happens every now and then," he remarked. "Just as well to keep out of it."

As they neared the corner, Elizabeth glanced back. A crowd had gathered. Two sergents-de-ville walked toward the scene with impressive, unhurried strides, stroking their mustaches.

Elizabeth and her companion walked up the Boulevard du Montparnasse to the *Closerie des Lilas.* There they drank sweet liqueurs under the trees, looking out over the Avenue de l'Observatoire to the battered walls of the old Bal Bullier. Afterwards, they took a taxi back to Cross's studio.

CHAPTER 13.

Wherein Mr. Quimby Dabbles With the Tip of One Finger in the Sacred Fount.

As the result of skillful maneuver, Mr. Willoughby Quimby found himself seated one warm night on the terrace of the Café des Deux Maggots, alone with Lucille Grosvenor and two coffees.

Opposite them, with classic simplicity of design, a round white moon was located in measured juxtaposition to the stark, square tower of the Église Saint-Germain-des-Prés. The weathered stones were black against the profound color of the evening. A tattered wisp of cloud, caught on one of the moon's rays, floated without motion behind the tower. The composition was almost artificial in its perfection—a sort of celestial stage-setting.

Mr. Quimby always felt an imminent sense of medievalism in the relentless outlines of Saint-Germain-des-Prés. The gray old church, placidly oblivious to the city that had grown about it, seemed persistent harbor for the embers of an outgrown monasticism. The glare and merriment of modern Paris could not jar its repose, — seemed scarcely discordant. After all, was not this the very essence of medievalism — the chill architectural chastity a symbol of the realities of a harsh epoch against which humanity struggled into the release of color and laughter? Mr. Quimby dreamed of the rugged, imperishable stone of old churches, castles, cloisters, with the kaleidoscope of all that was most fleeting in gaiety and brilliance playing about them. That curious paradox of the middle age —the austerity of stone walls and an inflexible church as background to the brightest, lightest pageant of humanity that ever blazed on the canvas of the world—seemed to him oddly preserved in this stone heritage of another era

132

planted harmoniously in the heart of the most civilized city in Western Europe.

The conversation of Mr. Quimby with Lucille had consisted largely of tastefully disposed monosyllables on his part, punctuating the young woman's recurrent exuberant superlatives. The fact, found Mr. Quimby, that the prospect of church and moon and sky and trees and boulevard was "entrancing," that a vagrant amateur of cigarette butts was "too pathetic," that a bareheaded Gallic Viking in an opera cloak was "adorable looking," that the shamelessly amorous couple at the next table were "too cunning for words," conveyed unmeasured delight to the jaded emotions of Mr. Quimby. In every adolescent rapture he tasted newly of the fountain of youth.

Mr. Quimby had no less recently than that afternoon devoted some attention to his aspect as presented in the unimpeachable depths of his mirror. The procedure had caused him no small discomfort. His surfaces he found to be of deplorably uneven contour. He sagged where

133

every canon of comeliness demanded a pleasant firmness. Pouches under the eyes were not merely a superfluous adjunct, they were positively not prepossessing. Dexterous application of lotions might eliminate the occasional gray from his hirsute parts, but he felt no confidence in any elixir to restore hair to those regions whence it had seen fit to take its leave. His hands, too, were not agreeable. They were soft, yielding members, adapted to no more rigorous service than the practiced elevation of a tumbler. Assuredly, reflected Mr. Quimby without pleasure, he had ceased to be a spectacle adapted to the enjoyment of the feminine vision. Youth, he was forced to acknowledge, had surreptitiously taken leave of him. Circumstances being such as they were, he found the fact a melancholy one. The external deficiencies of Mr. Quimby were tonight, however, in marked contrast to his spiritual juvenility. The years which had affixed their indelible mark to his features seemed to have left invincible boyhood in his bosom.

He inhaled deeply of the nocturnal springtime. He thrilled in sentimental response to the white purity of the evening. For the first time he seemed to cast an emotional bridge over the river of years and experience that separated him from his daughter's friend. Tonight he was close to Lucille Grosvenor. He felt a possibility of intimate communion with this incomparable young person, the poetry of darkling Paris a kindly ambassador of rejuvenated maturity to untrammeled youth.

Now, Mr. Quimby was not a reticent gentleman. He was by nature communicative. A thought or a mood clamored within him for immediate expression. It was a part of his eminently social character that he could not, by the very nature of his intelligence, refrain from the prompt verbalization of whatever at any given moment chanced to be uppermost in his thought. The fact that for the first time in many sordid years a young and delicate and wholly charming emotion had become the chief factor in his mental life, arbitrarily called for vocal affirmation.

He honestly fought the impulse. He was quite conscious of the ignoble figure he would present in the guise of a diffident Romeo. But his impulses were too strong for him. He was unused to the exercise of restraint. The best he could do was to temper his potentially tempestuous avowal with a mild indirection.

"There is," he announced, characteristically garbing his meaning in a volume of words, "no limit to the idiotic aspects in which a moon and a good dinner will present an otherwise normal individual. Tonight I feel as I haven't felt for—well, since I was not much older than you. And the worst of it is that I shall probably not be able to hold my tongue about it and will only contrive to furnish a living illustration of the unkind truths voiced by the coiners of vest pocket sagacity about 'an old fool.'"

"You aren't," replied Lucille, very sensibly, "either a fool or—very—old. So I don't see what you're talking about."

Mr. Quimby groaned.

"Unhappily, my dear child, you very soon will see, such is the incontinence of my tongue. And, having seen, you will be forced to the conclusion that I am not only—rather—old, but that I am as complete and abject a fool as Paris at this time harbors."

"I don't think I'll be forced to that conclusion at all. But I do wish you'd tell me what you mean."

Mr. Quimby knocked the ash discreetly from the top of his cigarette. He devoted a long time to the ceremony.

"I have come," said he reluctantly, "to that epoch known leniently as the afternoon of life. Even, I may add, the late afternoon—life's tea-time, let us say. And, instead of tea, I have suddenly come to feel a shameless craving for the wine of youth. You'll forgive the somewhat tangled metaphor."

"It doesn't seem to me that a preference for wine over tea is a very striking new departure for you, is it?"

"There is," rejoined Mr. Quimby didactically, "wine. Also, there is wine."

"Oh!"

"In short, I find myself unready to resign my well-worn appetite to the salts and spices adapted to the palate of middle age. I feel striving within me a yearning—which should long since have perished—for the luscious, bountiful sweets denied my gray hairs."

"I don't see why you persist in this delusion of senility. But I wish you'd come to the point—if there is a point."

"Briefly, the point is this: A man of my years, of my pursuits, of my shape, of my tastes, has not the least right to caste himself in the fantastic role of amorous youth. That is to say, I can hardly tell even you, who are the most warmly sympathetic of mortals, that I am, naïvely and splendidly and hopelessly, in love, without presenting a picture of surpassing absurdity, without subjecting myself to your enchanting ridicule."

Lucille's wide brown eyes were fixed on him in a glow of pleasure. She was

138

dressed in brown, too, with a little brown *cloche* hat on her brown hair.

"Nothing of the sort," she exclaimed. "I wouldn't laugh at you for a minute. I think it's the most delightful thing in the world! I can't think of anything sweeter. Have you really fallen in love? It's too adorable of you!"

"There you are!" wailed Mr. Quimby, dismally. "That's exactly what I mean. You think it's adorable of me, and you think I'm a sweet thing, and you'd like to pat me on the head and tell your friends about me—and what good does all that do me? The extraordinary thing about a dilatory passion like mine is that it works just exactly like the love affairs of any blooming youth with the scars of his first razor fresh on his cheek. We patriarchal swains, too, are anxious not for the sympathy of our juniors; we want our devotion returned. We want our suit to be successful. We want not only to love, but to be loved back at! When rejected with sympathetic comment, we feel distinctly put out about it. And, anyway, we can't even go to the length of uncovering our fatuous egos to the extent of an avowal. So we have not even the wholesome melancholy of unsuccessful courtship, because courtship itself is denied us."

"I don't see why! You're not, as I think I pointed out, at all old. And you're very attractive and rich and kind-hearted. I don't see why you shouldn't win almost any unattached affections."

Mr. Quimby fondled his stomach tenderly. It had served him well, that expansive middle. He harbored towards it no resentment. Only a solemn regret.

"Here," said he mournfully, "in the very center of me, is the outward and deplorably visible symbol of the passing of my charm for the budding female."

"Don't be silly! Loads of girls fall in love with older and fatter and wickeder and poorer men than you. But I wish you'd tell me if you really are in love."

"Alas!" assented Mr. Quimby. "Such is the laughable case."

"With someone I know?"

"With someone you know."

"Tell me who!" she coaxed, leaning towards him.

Mr. Quimby felt childish and ill-at-ease. The colloquy was taking a form painfully reminiscent of his distant adolescence.

"That, I fear, I must decline to do."

"Why? I wouldn't think of saying a word! And I haven't a notion of laughing at you. I might be able to help."

"With a girl young enough to be my granddaughter?"

"How old is she?"

"Suppose she was about your age? Don't you see how silly my position really is?"

"No, I don't. Love isn't ever silly," sagely announced Miss Grosvenor.

"Suppose," Mr. Quimby's renascent youth had taken the bit in its teeth and bolted. He stammered on with his alcoholic heart beating furiously. "Suppose she were about your age, tall and warm and eager, with a brown frock and a silly little brown hat, and a great mass of

141

brown hair with two huge brown eyes looking at me from under it over a greasy café table. Suppose all that, and perceive, out of the utter wisdom of your youth, the majestic farce of my belated romanticism!"

The brown eyes quivered, opened wide in surprise, fell for a minute to the coffee on the table, sought refuge in the moonlit beauty of Saint-Germain-des-Prés. Lucille's cheeks were very faintly flushed. After a moment she answered, softly.

"I don't think it's a farce at all. I think it's perfectly beautiful and I'm enormously complimented. And I don't think it's a bit nice of you to talk as if you were ashamed of it. I'm very fond of myself, too, so that gives us something in common."

Mr. Quimby turned on her his woeful face.

"Well, there you are. I've done it. You see, now, what a charming muddle I've got myself into."

"I don't think it's a muddle," she looked at him earnestly. "Of course—of

142

course—I can't say that—right now, I—
er—feel that way about you—"

"Of course," murmured Mr. Quimby.

"Or that I ever will—"

"Of course," murmured Mr. Quimby.

"But," she brightened perceptibly,
"that's no reason at all for you to feel any
differently. I love to be loved, and I like
you a lot, and I think it's terribly nice of
you to feel that way about me. And some
day—well, you never can tell what *might*
happen."

"No," agreed her companion. "It's
far better not to tell what might happen."

"And I'm so glad you told me. It
makes things ever so much nicer—"

"Doesn't it?" Mr. Quimby smiled an
unusual smile.

"I'm glad you agree with me. And it
would have been a shame for you to have
kept it to yourself and never to have
realized how I felt. You might have
been dreadfully unhappy."

"Whereas now," he pronounced affa-
bly, "I am in one of the first seven heav-

ens of triumphant courtship. Let's change the subject."

"All right," doubtfully. "Though I don't think it's such a bad subject. And please don't stop loving me, will you?" she finished with a brilliant smile.

"What," irrelevantly remarked Mr. Quimby, "is my daughter doing these days? I see very little of her."

A shadow crossed Lucille's smooth brow, under the hat and the fringe of brown har.

"I don't really know. I'm a little worried. I haven't seen Betty very much either. Don't you think she is too much with this Mr. Cross? Is he quite—I mean—all right?"

Mr. Quimby, too, looked disturbed.

"No," said he. "Mr. Cross is not at all—all right. Perhaps I had better do something about it. In fact—I will do something about it."

There was a long, awkward silence. And then Lucille's irrepressible superlatives cleared the air of all save moonlight and the rattle of the city.

CHAPTER 14.

The Admirable Joseph is Confronted With Perplexities.

ELIZABETH was out when Mr. Quimby got up on the following morning. With her she took a small black dressing case, a motoring coat, a flush of perturbed anticipation. Her message, delivered to Mr. Quimby by the zealous Joseph, implied a week-end trip to the battle-fields with some friends—the Benjamins. Mr. Quimby received the news vaguely, mentally contemplated the opulently maternal Mrs. Benjamin and her obtrusively filial daughter, pondered Elizabeth's new-born toleration of their smugness, dismissed the matter with a weary shrug. He was in despondent mood, was Willoughby Quimby. He felt old and nervous and insatiable. He wanted something—a great deal of something—and he was neurotically impatient to find out what it was. So he acquiesced absently, donned hat and coat. The responsibilities of his daughter's upbringing remained for him a purely intellectual concept. He had not gone beyond a mental self-promise to "do something about the girl" one of these days.

He went out, leaving Joseph sole lord of his household.

That swarthy personage, his features contorted with acute dissatisfaction, busied himself about his domestic functions. Things were not to his liking. Faultless servant, his own nervous organization reflected the disorder of his master's. The old, assured, material, contented conduct of life which had possessed these rooms before the arrival of the young woman had been supplanted by an indecisive discomfort. New elements had been introduced — material and spiritual elements. Joseph, with his master, had been content in the *status quo*.

Any change, any contrast, was to be deplored.

So Joseph wagged his head and went disconsolately about his business. Captain Stirling called up to ask if Miss Grosvenor were there. Mr. Fletcher called up to ask if Mr. Quimby were there. Emilia, the neighboring Italian serving wench, called up to exchange amorous greetings with him, Joseph. Several hours passed without event. Joseph stepped out to dine at a neighboring café with an acquaintance. Together they lingered for an hour or two, moving from *bistro* to *bistro,* as they proceeded from cigarette to cigarette. At about eleven o'clock Joseph returned to the apartment. As he unlocked the service door, he could hear the telephone bell in Mr. Quimby's study. Shutting the door hastily, he hurried in, checked the persistent ringing by raising the 'phone to his ear and ventured a receptive "Hallo!"

The answering voice was peremptory and perceptibly agitated. Joseph recog-

147

nized it as that of Mr. Frederick
Fletcher.

"*C'est toi,* Joe?"

"*Mais oui,* M. Fletcher."

"*M. Quimby?*"

"*Il est sorti.*"

"*Où?*"

"*Ca, je ne sais pas.* M. Quimby left
no instructions."

"Do you know where I can find Mlle.
Grosvenor?"

Joseph shrugged and grimaced at the
telephone.

"How should I know, Monsieur? Unless indeed Mademoiselle is at home?"

"Where is that?"

"With her parents, Monsieur. The
number is Louvre 03-22."

"Louvre 03-22. Thanks. If you see
either M. Quimby or Mlle. Grosvenor,
have them call me at my place at once."

"*Entendu,* M. Fletcher."

Joseph replaced the telephone on its
rack and sighed heavily. Before the recent cataclysmic changes in the household, Mr. Fletcher would never have

been so agitated. Mr. Fletcher was never
so agitated. It was unheard of. These
women had brought with them only disorder and distress.

A violent ring at the door-bell, a
half-hour later, was Joseph's next inter-
ruption. The door opened, Lucille Grosvenor burst in, her wide, innocent eyes
dark with troubled excitement.

"Mr. Quimby?"

"Has not come in, Mademoiselle," said
Joe patiently.

"Where can I reach him? It is of the
most vital importance that I should get
him."

"Who shall say, Mademoiselle? M.
Quimby left no instructions. M. Fletcher
has been trying to reach both M. Quimby
and you, Mademoiselle. He wishes you
to call him."

"I have no time! I *must* reach Mr.
Quimby," she broke in. "For the love of
God, tell me where he *might* be."

Her brown eyes drove Joseph's rather
muddled thoughts to violent effort.

"Perhaps if Mademoiselle were to call

Élysées 55-55. It is a bar occasionally
frequented by M. Quimby. But he has
not been there very lately, I believe."

This counsel cost Joseph much mental
pain. He was aware that in the event of
Mr. Quimby's being at Dan's, it would
be a dire indiscretion to have revealed
that fact to Miss Grosvenor. But Joseph's
discretion was not proof against the evi-
dence of extreme urgency which he
found in Lucille's face.

Dan, answering the 'phone, explained
that Mr. Quimby was not there. Had he
been there? Dan hesitated, but sensing
tragedy in Lucille's tones, he, too, cast
discretion to the winds. Mr. Quimby
had left an hour earlier. Where was he
now? Dan did not know. Where *might*
he be? Almost anywhere. Mr. Quimby,
at midnight, was unpredictable. But Lucille was not to be appeased. She begged,
she stormed, she pleaded. She scolded
and she cajoled. She solemnly averred
that Mr. Quimby himself would see the
importance of her communication. Finally Dan, calling the Saints to witness

his misgivings, suggested a number which *might* reach Mr. Quimby. He had not said he would be there. But Dan had known Mr. Quimby many years. There he *might* be. Lucille expressed concise gratitude and rang off.

In a moment she called the number Dan had given her. Joseph hearing it, paled, and his face was knotted with acute foreboding. His indiscretion had magnified itself to preposterous proportions.

CHAPTER 15.

The Decline and Fall of Willoughby Quimby.

MR. WILLOUGHBY QUIMBY, in short, had lowered the flag of his conscientious paternity. He had permitted himself a brief, half-hearted appearance in the precincts of Dan's at the most perilous of hours—the period consecrated to the conscientious whetting of appetite. He was still in that nervous, despondent, dyspeptic mood occasioned as much by the discontinuance of his alcoholic ration as by the amiable rebuff to his amorous hopes; as much by the sudden alteration of his agreeably dissolute way of life as by the eruption of responsible parenthood. Lounging listlessly about the bar-room, he encountered acquaintance upon acquaintance. His persistent refusal of refreshment began to lose conviction. The inevitable "one cocktail" was finally yielded to, absorbed, relished. The exception was extended to a second, to a third. The aspect of the world grew increasingly congenial. Stars became accessible. Lucille was observed in her true place—a pleasantly silly fancy. He was well out of the affair. The obligations of fatherhood became no more than cloudy specters on a roseate alcoholic horizon. Dan's place lost the aspect of temptation, became an embattled citadel for the harassed temperament. The people about him ceased to appear to him as drunken acquaintances to be shunned. They became the boon companions of a wider life. Mr. Quimby found himself again in the environment for which he felt that his destiny designed him. A great glow of delighted liberty enlivened him, coursed through his veins. He became unwontedly garrulous. He absorbed every fragment of the esoteric gossip of the Paris bars. He renewed old associations, drank old toasts, revived old sensations.

Mr. Quimby dined alone at one of his favorite restaurants. He permitted himself a repast that would have shamed Lucullus. He accompanied it with a renowned wine. He punctuated it finally with a brandy so dignified by years and origin as to be served him with an almost cringing reverence.

When Mr. Quimby arose from the table, his pleasure had passed even the bounds of satisfaction. He was replete; he was exuberant. The past had become a golden haze; the future a path of rose-leaves. The present alone was real to him, and the present was no more than a jumble of agreeable physical impressions. He was forced to concentrate a little on the precision of his words, on the accuracy of his step, on the focus of his gaze. He toyed with more than his usual nervousness with the thinning grayish hair.

CHAPTER 16.

Mr. Quimby Continues to Fall.

IT was late when Mr. Quimby left the restaurant—too late for the theatre, even had his condition admitted that form of amusement. He was alone, but his potations had engendered a need for convivial intercourse. It was too early for the *boites de nuit*. Mr. Quimby repaired in a taxi to Dan's for further consideration of his dilemma.

Dan's was practically deserted. Mr. Quimby devoted a half hour to conversation alone with the presiding genius of the place. It was one of those curious, incomparable, endless, futile, emphatic discussions which exist only between bartenders of genius and those of their clients who are able to show the visible manifestation of that genius.

Gradually, in the submerged intelligence of Mr. Quimby, in that obscure region of his mind which was not occupied with Dan's discourse, there began to grow and to burn and finally to blaze, an obsessing idea—an insidious, overwhelming suggestion. Mr. Quimby was experiencing a sudden relief—a new liberty. He felt not unlike one who has suddenly awakened from a dream of bondage. He was not a young enough man to change his life, he reasoned. And now, suddenly, mysteriously, through the agency of a few drinks, he found himself again with the world at his feet. The disturbing window opened into another life—other ideals, other dreams, other ambitions— was blurred into a glow of alcohol. What, after all, had he to do with fatherhood, with the saccharine heartbreaks of emotions he had long outgrown? What, indeed, was he to find in dim notions of regeneration, of a domestic old age, of temperance, of ambition? His life had ordered itself otherwise, and he had never been discontented. Life was a thing to be lived in the enjoyment of the present. Regret for the past, hope for the future—these were irrelevant fancies of the superstitious or the cowardly.

Tonight, resolved Mr. Quimby (and the blood pulsed furiously under the gray-sprinkled hair of his temples), tonight he would free himself once and for all of the notions engendered by the cataclysmic descent upon his life's ordered disorder of his daughter and her disastrous friend. The corollary, he reflected in a rush of half terrified excitement, was inevitable. There was one fit gesture alone that would serve to celebrate his return to the existence of whose art he was master. He found a pleasurable terror in the contemplation of it—renascence of a sensation of guilt and agitation he had thought himself to have long outgrown.

Mr. Quimby paid for his drinks, said good night to Dan, tipped the *chasseur* who called him a taxi; stepped into it with a cautious dignity of demeanor.

The address he gave was not far from the opera.

A sudden revulsion of feeling, a temptation to change his direction, brought him to the window of the cab. But Mr. Quimby was not a determined man. He relaxed again, his heart throbbing with a curious medley of emotions. He resolutely refused to permit himself a thought of either his daughter or Lucille Grosvenor. Instead, he devoted such of his attention as he could command to the meticulous adjustment of his necktie, of the protruding corner of his handkerchief, of his boutonnière.

A sleepily irate concierge changed to a cringing bundle of smiles at sight of him. The maintenance of Georgette's apartment had entailed the dispensing, with Mr. Quimby's characteristic generosity, of considerable largess. Yes, Madame was in her rooms. She was, he added,— Mr. Quimby felt unnecessarily,—alone. Was he to announce the visitor? Mr. Quimby rather haughtily pointed out that that had never been the custom in

the past. The concierge shrugged his
shoulders, raised his eyebrows, returned
to his disrupted slumbers. Mr. Quimby
proceeded upwards in the one-way lift.

The stuffy interior of the building af-
fected him unpleasantly. He shut his
eyes for a moment and his head swam dis-
astrously. Mr. Quimby shook himself,
took himself resolutely in hand. When
he rang Georgette's doorbell he was ex-
ternally as cold and sober as he was fastidiously clad.

There was a pause, a few unidentifi-
able sounds. Mr. Quimby did not quite
rock on his feet. Finally the door
opened. Georgette, a dressing-gown hastily thrown over her nightdress, her fair,
short hair a tangle of curls about her face,
confronted him in sleepy surprise.

"Tiens! C'est toi! What are you doing
here at this hour of the night?"

Mr. Quimby got his tongue under control with an effort. This was not precisely the welcome he had expected, but
he replied affectionately.

159

"I could stay away no longer, my darling. May I come in?"

"If you like."

Georgette turned impatiently and led the way. Mr. Quimby sank contentedly into the easy-chair which had in the past been his accustomed one. He lit a cigarette. So did his hostess. She flung the contents of an ash tray into the fireplace. Mr. Quimby, with fleeting suspicion, fancied he caught a glimpse of cigarette-butts of an unaccustomed brand. He dismissed the notion. She was a good girl, Georgette. So long as it was he who paid her bills, even in his absence he felt that her fidelity could be relied on.

"Well? And where is your daughter?"

"My daughter?" Mr. Quimby made an effort to order his thoughts. "Oh, my daughter. Let us not think of her. We are alone again, Georgette, my love. Alone again, together, at last!"

Georgette looked closely into his eyes.

"You're drunk!" she pronounced.

He debated the wisdom of denial, and shrugged his shoulders.

"If you like."

"And what now?"

"What now? Am I not welcome?"
Georgette flew into a sudden passion.
"Welcome? *Ah, b'en alors! Là tu va fort!* Welcome indeed! You think you can arrive at any time of night and find me with no idea but to take you in my arms? One is no longer permitted to sleep, hein?"

"In the old days I did not have to pick the hour of my visits," murmured Mr. Quimby. But he, too, mingled with his awakened desires, began to feel a touch of resentment. Georgette made an impatient gesture with her cigarette.

"Then it was different. You were expected. One could be prepared. If you can live so contentedly without me for so long, you can at least return to me sober and at a sensible hour."

"Nevertheless, I am still your friend."
The phrase was ill chosen. His companion's eyes flashed.

"You mean that you still support me? To hell with your support! Throw me

161

out tomorrow and you will see how long I shall be alone!"

A disturbing suspicion returned to Mr. Quimby's mind. He spoke hesitatingly.

"You have perhaps already found my successor? Is it because you feared I might interrupt a—rendezvous?"

Georgette answered only with a scornful glance. Mr. Quimby rose, a little unsteadily. He paused for a moment, trying to think. Then he threw his cigarette into the hearth, shrugged his shoulders, and turned to the door.

"Then," said he, with a faint smile, "There remains to me but one course. I shall relieve you of my—inopportune presence. Good night, Georgette!"

Georgette bit her pretty lip, gazing at the hand he outstretched. It was a warm, pleasantly furnished little flat, this one he had given her. Suddenly she seized his hand, raising softened blue eyes.

"Come, my little Willy! I ask your pardon. I am hasty, because I am sleepy. Forgive me—*tu veux?* Last night I slept badly, *viens, mon petit gros—Viens à Georgette!"*

Mr. Quimby tugged perplexedly at his hair. He felt that a protest was the course most compatible with his dignity. But Georgette's touch was persuasive. It quickened his already burning pulse. Besides, it was nice here. He was not anxious to go farther, and the rounded invitation of Georgette's fragrant little body, the appeal of her caressing gaze, were imperious. Relaxing his resistance, he let himself be replaced in his chair, a great final thrill of physical anticipation making his heart bound. Georgette kissed him, hotly and fully on his lips and then straightened up.

"Whisky-soda?" suggested Georgette, sweetly.

CHAPTER 17.

Whereupon Miss Elizabeth Quimby
Passes an Unpleasant Evening.

THE swift Bugatti of Conway Cross deposited that polished gentleman and Elizabeth Quimby before the Hotel du Gd. Monarque at Chartres between five and six o'clock. Elizabeth, her great adventure clutched in trembling fingers, sank for a nervous instant into a chair on the central terrace of the Hotel while her companion assured himself of their reservation and while a perspiring youth staggered in with bags, coats, bundles. A swift glance assured the errant young woman that her chief dread—a familiar face—was not at once to confront them. Then they went upstairs.

Elizabeth's emotions on entering their spacious double room on the sunlit court were rather overpowering than clearly defined. She was white and she could not help trembling. This, it was brought home to her with an unanticipated force, was a very different matter from the discreet intimacies of Cross's studio. To pass the threshold of a common sleeping apartment with a man who remained to her an almost perfect stranger was to destroy her established and ingrained viewpoint with a shattering blow. The door closed on all that she had ever experienced. For the first time she was filled with a consuming terror of the new world she had cloudily longed to know. This reality was so immediate, so concrete, and her dreams had been so pleasantly nebulous. She shook uncontrollably, and the artist took her smilingly into his arms. His deep voice made phrases which she remotely grasped. Unexpectedly, she wept, hiding her wet face in his shoulder, so that she did not see his impatient frown.

Finally, soothed by his embrace, by his strong voice, she smiled, a little feebly, through her tears. He breathed his relief and disengaged himself hastily. He disliked that sort of emotion. So he took his leave, promising to await her over an *apéritif* downstairs. Elizabeth sat on the edge of the bed for a few minutes, her heart beating against her breast. Her face was white and red, alternately. The day had been the most momentous not only that she had ever experienced, but even that she had ever conceived.

Cross's persistence and his curious, prevailing charm had at last, supported by the vitality of the rebellion that lay chained within her, persuaded her to a swift, delicious expedition. They had compromised on a one night's journey only—at most two—Cross yielding his week only after prolonged demur. They had chosen Chartres, despite the danger of encountering tourists who might know her, at her request. Elizabeth had a curious mystical feeling about the Cathedral. Under its shadow she felt stronger —surer of herself—less alone. It was an almost religious emotion, but one which she did not connect at all with the Chris-

tian significance of the building. It was
rather the feeling of permanent vitality
in its Gothic outlines, of calm defiant
splendor in the glow of its ancient glass,
of inscrutable solemnity in its deathless
sculpture. The riddle of life, she felt,
was enshrined in its sombre vault; the
carven saints and monarchs at its portals
could, if they would, voice the secret of
the sphinx.

They had lunched at a little outdoor
restaurant in a neighboring town, passed
the afternoon roaming along the twisted
streets of Chartres, up its sudden slopes,
over its crumbling bridges of stone. They
had looked along the stagnant banks of
the Eure at tumbled homes that seemed
built upon the green waters. They
had walked under the Porte Guillaume,
stood under the soaring buttresses of St.
Pierre and in the cool shade of St. Aig-
nan. They had passed little Gothic carv-
ings exhumed from the plaster of houses
planted askew on dizzy, cobbled declivi-
ties. They had wandered in the little
park behind the Cathedral, bought

photos from the little verger who was himself an artist, a vessel full to overflowing of the beauty of his regal charges —his photographs the overflow. They had sat in the car before the carven portals, meditated under the flaming windows. All this because Cross knew that in medieval art was one of his conversational fortes, and because Elizabeth was timidly—though unadmittedly—anxious to postpone their arrival at the hotel which was the curiously dreaded symbol of what she called her "adventure."

Elizabeth trembled still as she washed, and did eccentric feminine things to the mass of her dark hair. She was stifled by the sudden terror of life—of this maelstrom of life which she had permitted to take her in its grasp. She flung open the window and took a deep draft of the evening air.

The room was on the first floor and just over the central court of the hotel. Elizabeth saw Conway Cross sitting just below her, a glass of port on the table before him, looking calmly out over the

dusty square in front of the hotel. She
watched him for a long time, wondering
if the not very notable emotions aroused
by his somewhat unimpressive presence
were adequate to the occasion. At last
she turned from the window with a sigh
and redirected her attention to her mir-
rored image and the deft correction of
its deficiencies.

At last she felt herself prepared to resume the conduct of her experiment and
she, very hesitantly, left the room, walked
down the corridor and down the single
flight of stairs. Arrived in the small and
dingy lobby, Elizabeth paused in the
open doorway to take final stock of the
situation before joining her traveling
companion. She looked again at the table
where Cross had been sitting. There he
still was, his half empty port glass in his
hand. But—Elizabeth started back in
alarm—he was no longer alone!

Seated at the same table, their backs to
the doorway in which now stood Elizabeth, were a man and woman, dressed for
motoring. She could not see their faces,

169

but the brief survey was enough to show
her a stubby sort of a gentleman and a
commanding feminine colossus in a singularly ill-fitting American motoring
coat. Elizabeth drew back instinctively
and would have gone immediately to the
room, but that Cross had already seen
her.

"Hullo, Elizabeth!" he called, genially. "Come on over and join us. You
needn't be nervous—these people are old
friends of mine."

Very slowly, Elizabeth walked toward
them. Cross arose to greet her with a
comfortable smile.

"Let me present one of my newest and
—" with what may have been a discreet
leer—"one of my dearest friends, Miss
Quimby here, to two of my oldest and
surest friends—Mrs. Clark and Mr.
Koenig."

Mrs. Clark and Mr. Koenig greeted
Elizabeth with a wide and perspiring
cordiality.

"Hullo, dearie!" said Mrs. Clark, the
words issuing fulsomely from a wet and

170

flaccid mouth. "You needn't be scared of us; we're broad-minded, Joe and me. And it's not the first time we've been deaf and dumb for Conway!"

Cross broke in hurriedly.

"Yes, my dear Elizabeth," he remarked, with elaborate unconcern. "You may be sure that our friends understand that our little visit here is just what it seems—a trifling sight-seeing tour with the daughter of an old friend." He cleared his throat significantly.

Mr. Koenig here entered the discussion with a heavy chuckle and a heavier wink.

"That's it, Cross old boy! 'Just what it seems' is right, eh?" he nudged Cross with an elbow. "You old rascal, you!"

The countenance of Conway Cross began to lose its inflexible composure. He began to perceive his terrible, perhaps irretrievable, mistake. He bit his lips. It was not like him to commit so heinous a technical error. He started to speak again, but Mrs. Clark had come to the extreme limit of her clearly unaccus-

171

tomed silence. Cross lit a cigarette with nervous fingers.

"That's right, my dear!" said Mrs. Clark. "Joe and me are as mum as two water hydrants. And—" she lowered her voice playfully—"as a matter of fact, our own little tour is maybe—just a little bit—romantic too—eh? I mean—well —Joe and me ain't so young as you and Conway, but there is life in us two pups yet! And since I had my face lifted—"

"Whoever lifted your face, Moll," wise-cracked Mr. Koenig, "must have let go and dropped it on a pile of rocks!"

Elizabeth was standing, absolutely motionless, the black hair beneath her little hat surrounding the blank pallor of her face. For a moment she thought herself on the point of fainting. Then a sudden cool rush of anger steadied her, strengthened her. Her brain tightened in a hard knot of resentment. Her limbs were numb, her heart paralyzed. But she was cold, cold as ice, cold as death.

She had not thought of anything to say, but a curious innate self-possession—per-

172

haps a gift from her father—came to her rescue. Suddenly her rigid body relaxed and her slow, feline smile turned the corners of her mouth.

"Thank you, Conway," she murmured, "for introducing your friends. Already I owe them very much. They have taught me something. I am going now. Good day, Mrs. Clark, Mr. Koenig. And"—very deliberately — "Good-by, Conway."

She turned and lounged out of the hotel with inimitable self-possession. Cross stood, dumbfounded and horrified.

Elizabeth collapsed a few minutes after she had crossed the threshold. Hot tears streaked her cheeks and she nearly ran through the darkening streets, trying to hide her eyes in a square inch of handkerchief.

Always Elizabeth had known that she was not the first woman in Cross's life. Nor, indeed, the twentieth. A part of the zest of the episode grew from that very fact. What she sought was very emphatically not the delicate savor of untrammeled romance. She wanted passion—experienced, knowing passion. But she had looked too for something beyond. The concept of her great adventure was inextricably mingled with the eternally vital forces of life. She asked for a cosmic emotion. She had not clearly defined her wants. She dared not analyze her hunger, perhaps because she knew that it would not bear analysis. But she did quite clearly know that she had not thought of her adventure—either in general or in this particular manifestation— as a mere week-end liaison. She had not tried to grasp fully the elaborate phrases of Conway Cross. She had let herself be swept by them into a dream of amorous ecstacy.

And now it had suddenly been brought to her already harassed understanding that the episode was only grand in its phrasing. The episode just passed added nothing to her knowledge of her position. Nothing was altered. It was not the indelicacy of Cross's revelation of her identity to which she objected chiefly. That she could condone. But to have her romance tossed loosely into a category of petty seduction turned the brand in her bosom. Her great adventure became a sordid game. Having conceived herself as a consuming flame of love, she had suddenly heard herself classed as the victim of an habitual seducer. By an accident of verbal approach, her excursion with Conway Cross had ceased to be a triumph of pride and had become a burning indignity. The dignifying phrases had been stripped from the humiliating void of her folly.

So Elizabeth wept and walked quickly through the darkling streets of Chartres. Instinctively she turned her steps toward the Cathedral, stalwart symbol of consolation and protection. Her tears flowed no longer when, a little breathless, she came out upon the little square and looked up at the two spires surging against the stars. Aspiration, hope, a soaring into the mysterious divinity of the future—in these she found the strength to meet the present, to face the sudden falling away of the deceptively firm ground of her illusion.

She sat for a few moments on a bench, breathing heavily, without thought of what her next move should be. Then she walked slowly toward the Cathedral, around to the gloomy east portals. The building was closed, but Elizabeth sank wearily on the steps. She no longer felt any inclination to weep nor even to think. She felt the comforting companionship of the ancient carven beings about her. Their placid wisdom enveloped her in a cool wave of contemplative quiescence. So she sat for a long time, neither planning, nor hoping, nor fearing.

The lights of a motor car swept across the square in front of the Cathedral, up to its gates. Elizabeth heard, remotely, the motor shut off. A door slammed and a shadowy figure came around the corner of the Cathedral. She heard a quick step on the pavement and Conway Cross stood over her. His voice, tuned to a careful agitation, came to her as from a great distance.

"I say, Elizabeth! I am sorry. I behaved like a scoundrel. I had no right to let you meet those people. But I had no idea—I didn't realize how completely horrible it would be. Can you possibly forgive me?"

His manner was pleading but confident. Elizabeth rose suddenly, her meditation disrupted, her whole mind filled with rebellion against the episode he represented. She stood tall and languid, with a curious, lazy fire in her eyes.

"Please go away and leave me alone," she said, her voice flat and toneless. Cross came a step nearer.

"Don't be silly, Elizabeth. You'll catch your death of cold sitting here. Come back to the hotel—won't you? I have apologized—sincerely. And I can solemnly assure you that those people will never mention the incident to anyone. Nor will I. You can surely rely on me for that, can't you?"

Elizabeth spoke with an effort. It was all so clear to her. Why did she have to explain? Why did she have to try to

177

put it into words? Why wouldn't he go
—and leave her?

"You don't understand," her voice was
more husky than ever. "It's not meeting
them. That doesn't matter. Only you
have put the whole thing on a different
basis for me. You have shown me what
you are—a peculiarly unsavory sort of
a swine. Not that I hold that against
you. With your material assistance I've
made a fool of myself. I suppose, from
your point of view, you had a right to
take advantage of my idiocy. But now,
if you'll forgive my saying so, I loathe
you more than anything in the world."

Cross was taken aback. But he was
gifted with a swift and supple intelligence. He bowed a little humbly.

"I understand. You have cleared
away the mists of rather absurd romanticism and have seen our little expedition
a little more—crudely, shall I say? But
that does not in any way alter the matter
fundamentally. Here we are, you and
I—man and woman. Fate has placed
us here, alone. Why should a difference

178

in wording—in point of view, if you like, affect our conduct? Why should I not take you in my arms here as well as in my studio?"

"Still you don't understand. And I don't really see why I should go to the trouble of making you. You have made what I conceived, what you led me to conceive, as high romance, into cheap intrigue. You have put it on a par with a back stairs petting party. You have extracted the spirit and left only the flesh. So I wish you would go and leave me."

She leaned against an iron railing and passed her hand wearily over her white brow. Cross leaned forward, his eyes hot.

"There it is you who fail to understand —who are wrapping reality in phrases. Do you want me to tell you what the reality is? It is this:—That we want each other, Elizabeth! I want to hold you and feel the blood hot in your veins and the breath hot in your lungs. And that is all that matters. The rest is nothing."

Elizabeth trembled a little, but her lazy voice was assured with that strange, courageous assurance that rarely deserted her. She answered him with a twist of a smile on her lips.

"You put it attractively, Conway. But one thing you have overlooked in the enthusiasm of your desire. It may be very true that you 'want' me with so superlative a wanting. But I, on the other hand, happen to want nothing so much as never to see you again!"

Cross put a tense hand on her arm.

"You fool!" he snapped, angrily. "You don't know what you're talking about. Give me a kiss and don't talk so much."

He took her suddenly in his arms. Elizabeth pushed him back with all her strength.

"You beast!" she panted.

"We are both beasts!" he exulted. "And that is why we want each other. And that is why we are going back to the hotel!"

A quiet voice broke in from close beside them. They had been too absorbed to hear the step of a newcomer who now stood tall and gaunt on the dark steps.

"Good evening, Conway!" said the voice, pacifically. "Hullo, Elizabeth! A little difference of opinion?"

They turned to face the figure behind them.

"Freddy Fletcher!" exclaimed Elizabeth.

Cross took a step backwards.

"How are you, Fletcher?" he remarked, coolly.

Mr. Frederick Fletcher took Elizabeth's arm, smiling cheerfully.

"My car is around the corner. Come on, Elizabeth. We're going back to Paris!"

"You'll oblige me," said Cross, deliberately, "by removing yourself, Fletcher. Elizabeth isn't going back to Paris."

"I haven't the slightest desire to oblige you, Conway," murmured Freddy

Fletcher, amiably. "And Miss Quimby *is* going back to Paris!"

He took Elizabeth by the arm and led her quietly down the steps. Cross leaped after them and stopped short as Fletcher turned.

"I'll make you regret this, young man!" snapped Cross angrily.

"Yes?" said Mr. Frederick Fletcher, as he turned away with his companion.

CHAPTER 18.

And Mr. Quimby Plumbs the Depths.

MR. WILLOUGHBY QUIMBY awoke to find his rotund form being violently agitated by his hostess. He blinked some half dozen times, passed a hand nervously through his hair, came sharply to the consciousness of a piercing headache and inordinately weighted eyelids. The apartment was lit by a single shaded lamp, but the light thrust into his hot eyes like a needle. He licked dry lips with a dry tongue.

"Quick, quick, *mon ami!* It is for you—the telephone. I think it is perhaps your daughter!" The voice was Georgette's.

Mr. Quimby gazed at her in surprise, struggled to a realization of his position.

"For me? But—how the devil does anyone know I'm here?"

183

"That makes no difference. It has already been ten minutes that I have been waking you. Go quickly and see what it is."

Mr. Quimby heaved himself wearily from the bed, yawned, flung a sheet majestically about his pudgy body, and strode to the 'phone.

"Hallo! . . . Yes—this is Willoughby Quimby. . . . My God!"

Mr. Quimby nearly let the instrument fall. His puffy cheeks were a blotched crimson. Remotely, cloudily, he heard Lucille's voice:

"Oh, Mr. Quimby, it's too awful! Elizabeth has disappeared, and Mr. Fletcher says he thinks she has gone to Chartres with that Cross man! You must do something right away. It's horrible!"

Mr. Quimby struggled to control his voice and stammered thickly from his dry throat.

"What—! Elizabeth — Chartres — Cross—My God! All right—I'll see to it. You're sure about Chartres?"

184

"Mr. Fletcher says he knows Mr. Cross left for there in his car, with someone. And Elizabeth was seen with him just before he left. Mr. Fletcher said he might go down there himself. He was dreadfully upset."

"Tell Fletcher it's none of his business. I'll—I'll leave at once. I'll be in Chartres inside of two hours. But how—," Willoughby Quimby's voice failed him and he dropped the telephone wearily on to its hook.

Georgette was watching him, curiously.

"What is it?" She asked. "Something serious?"

Willoughby Quimby made an impatient gesture.

"Nothing," said he shortly. "Only I must go—at once."

"But you are too tired, my little Willy! See—you can almost not keep your eyes open."

Mr. Quimby hardly heard her. He was consumed with shame. To be called up by the girl he loved and honored more

185

than anything in the world, to be told by her that through his negligence his daughter was at that very moment being betrayed and he in the arms of a woman who lived by her sold caresses! It was loathesome. He felt as though he had flung filth into Lucille's face and into his daughter's.

How had he come here, any way? The events of the evening were hazy in his memory. He had been drunk—still was, a little—stupidly, humiliatingly drunk. And this was the result.

Georgette pressed closely to him, looked with wide blue eyes into his watery ones.

"Kiss me, Willy," she murmured, smiling a little, caressingly.

He thrust her brutally away and flung himself down on the bed, hiding his burning face on the pillow. The sheet he had wrapped about him slipped unnoticed to the floor. He trembled and sobbed—wracking dry sobs. Little by little he grew calmer, but still he lay upon the bed. Finally his breathing

186

grew thick and rhythmic. It merged in a succession of harsh snores. Mr. Quimby slept.

Georgette's lip curled in distaste as she watched him. She turned out the light and lay down beside him. The room became still save for the snoring of Willoughby Quimby.

CHAPTER 19.

Willoughby Quimby Attains to a New Conception of Himself.

MR. QUIMBY awoke with a start and looked at his watch by the gray morning light. It was six o'clock. He leaped from the bed with a quick clutching pain at his heart. He was past cursing himself. It was too horrible. First the shame of Lucille's telephone call finding him here—here, of all places. And then the greater shame of having allowed himself to sleep again. He shuddered and passed a pudgy nervous hand over his pulsing brow. Then he splashed cold water on his face and began to dress hastily. Georgette still slept—the sound, untroubled slumber of the pure in heart, he reflected bitterly. Once dressed, he cast a last glance at her pretty, tranquil face amid its tumbled hair, and left the apartment. He was thinking quickly—a bit dizzily. Two ideas pounded in his brain. One was the imminent necessity of getting to Chartres—without delay. The other was a sudden surging hatred of Conway Cross—probably Mr. Quimby's first overwhelming emotion in years.

It was too early to get hold of his own chauffeur, so Mr. Quimby walked swiftly to a near-by garage. A brisk attendant recognized him with a smile.

"I can serve you, M. Quimby?"

"You still have the Hispano which I rented last month?"

"Monsieur is fortunate. The chauffeur has this moment arrived."

Mr. Quimby stopped first at his own flat. He let himself softly in with a key. Joseph he could hear rattling about in the kitchen. Mr. Quimby tip-toed into his own room, opened a drawer beside his bed and took out a small, black automatic pistol. His lips were set tightly, their grimness almost comically incongruous on his easy-going countenance. He re-

mained long enough to mix and drink a
bromo-seltzer, made his way noiselessly
to the door and five minutes later was
passing through the Porte d'Auteuil.

The Hispano limousine settled quietly
and smoothly down to the business of
getting Willoughby Quimby to Chartres
in the briefest possible space of time.
Inside the car, Mr. Quimby himself,
clutching the weapon in his pocket con-
vulsively, was torn by as confused a medley of frantic thoughts as he had ever
been a prey to. He felt that in one way
alone could he redeem himself, in one
way alone could he at least in part undo
the harm of his unspeakable negligence.
He had, with a thrill almost of pleasure,
cast off the garment of his sophistication.
He felt that he had become a man again.
He felt that he had become great in his
wrath. His daughter must, he resolved
frantically, be saved or avenged. That
Cross should have dared!—that he himself should have been lax enough to permit!—one idea pursued another and
massed into the total of his blind rage.

Almost, he said to himself, his life of anemic indulgence would be redeemed in this last assertion of sanguinary manhood. He closed his fist tightly on the pistol and his face was distorted with passion. He had not realized before what his fatherhood meant.

A good part of Mr. Quimby's indignation, be it said, was subconsciously directed at himself. But it found a natural outlet in his avenging anger at his daughter's traducer. He did not pause to formulate his approach to Conway Cross. He had decided vaguely that this was not an occasion for delicacy. His fury would find words for its expression. So he stared wildly at the straight yellow road ahead, with bleared and faded eyes, squeezed his pistol and from time to time tugged at his hair.

After a half hour, Mr. Quimby's reaction asserted itself and his head nodded on his breast. The grip on the automatic relaxed, and he slept a fitful, broken sleep. When he awoke, the car was at the door of the Grand Monarque.

Mr. Quimby's wrath came back with his senses, and with his wrath a sort of terror. With a heart furiously thumping and a disheveled appearance, he entered the hotel and walked to the desk. Again his hand closed tightly on the steel thing in his pocket.

A calculated *pour-boire* enabled Mr. Quimby to dispense with the formality of being announced. He ascended the one flight of stairs in a fever of hysterical wrath. His fingers ached with clutching his weapon. His temples throbbed painfully. At the top of the stairs he turned the wrong way and glowered fruitlessly at door after door until he had retraced his steps and identified that which he sought.

Mr. Quimby paused on the threshold and drew the automatic pistol. He contemplated it grimly. A neat, compact instrument of destruction. He permitted himself the luxury of anticipation. In his impassioned mind he saw himself in the doorway confronting Conway Cross. He saw himself as the avenger, as a cold

fury dealing ultimate justice from the
stubby barrel of the instrument in his
hand. Remotely he conceived his daughter in the background—cowering in mingled terror and awe. Mr. Quimby raised
his hand furiously to pound on the door.
And suddenly his heart turned to water
within him. The habit of thirty quiet,
urbane years fell upon him—a stifling
cloak. He was aghast at the thing he
had contemplated. Murder! That he,
pattern of tolerance, apostle of the easiest
way, should be so mastered by a passion
in its essence so utterly primeval! In the
passing of an instant Mr. Quimby became himself—again the acme of decadent civilization. His hour of fury had
passed and he turned from the exultant
avenger to the polished diplomat. Willoughby Quimby passed his hand uneasily through his gray hair, straightened his
tie, and rapped decorously. As an after
thought, he pocketed the pistol.

When Conway Cross, sleepy and re-
sentful in his mauve pyjamas, unlocked
and opened the door, Willoughby

Quimby still hovered on the border line
between vengeful anger and studied indifference. His nature and the posture
of his career triumphed, and his mien
was as courteously unruffled, his demeanor as undisturbed as though the
meeting were of the most casual.

"Well?" inquired Cross, irritably.

"Good morning!" vouchsafed Willoughby Quimby, with a cheery smile.
"May I come in?"

Cross stood aside without a word. Mr.
Quimby thereupon entered and glanced
quickly about the room. His face fell as
he became aware of his daughter's absence. Had he been misinformed? Had
the telephone call been a practical joke
—or a drastic chastisement for his be-
havior? He tugged at his hair. His
host extended a cigarette case. Willoughby Quimby took one with a bow.

"You will forgive my unseasonable
call, I'm sure, when I explain its character," he remarked, accepting a light
from Cross's enameled lighter. The artist
raised an eyebrow.

194

"Indeed?" he murmured, expectantly.

"I was led to believe that I should find my daughter in your company."

"I fear," said Conway Cross, courteously, "that you were misinformed."

"So it appears. You will allow me to apologize for my intrusion?" Mr. Quimby was still sorely perplexed, but relieved that he had replaced the pistol. Cross answered him with a gesture. Mr. Quimby was a little at a loss.

"Do you happen to know where Elizabeth actually is?"

"I have not the slightest idea," was the truthful reply.

Willoughby Quimby was thoroughly disconcerted. He was by this time firmly convinced that he had uncovered a mare's nest. The obvious course seemed to him to beat as graceful a retreat as possible.

"I'm sure you're in a hurry to redispose your limbs in slumber, Conway," he vouchsafed, genially. "So if you'll excuse me, I'll run along. Profuse apologies—and thanks for the cigarette."

"Not at all," Conway Cross's handshake was cordial, and he walked to the door. As Mr. Quimby was about to step through it, however, the other man stopped him, as by an after thought. "Oh—by the way, Quimby! Here's something you might care to take along."

Cross picked up, from a corner of the room, a small patent leather traveling bag on which Mr. Quimby recognized to his horror the initials "E. Q." For a fleeting instant his hand dropped again to his right hand coat pocket. And then his nature reasserted itself. With a pale face and a slightly unsteady hand he took the case, looked for a silent minute full into Cross's ironic eyes, and walked out of the room without a word.

CHAPTER 20.

A Proposition.

ELIZABETH lunched with Freddy Fletcher at Larue's. She was still tired and shaken by the events of the preceding day, but glad of a chance to order her thoughts and adjust her plans with one who was at once sympathetic and in possession of the facts. She had not yet seen her father—nor, for that matter, had any one else.

Freddy Fletcher ate for a long time in silence. He had hardly spoken on the drive back from Chartres, had proposed the meal in a noncommittal sentence,— had, in short, ably sustained his reputation for amiable taciturnity. Elizabeth talked nervously, irrelevantly. It was not until the *crème d'Isigny* had fallen like a succulent mantle upon the *petites fraises du bois* that she touched upon her midnight rescue.

"You must think I'm a peculiarly silly and rather disgusting young person, Freddy," she remarked, tentatively.

"On the contrary, I think you are a singularly courageous and notably fascinating individual."

"You'll at least grant that I've made a thoroughgoing fool out of myself."

"You couldn't do that. You've done a foolish thing—but only because its foolishness was not within the scope of your experience."

"What do you think I'd better do about it?"

"Nothing."

"What shall I tell my father?"

"Nothing."

"What shall I say to Conway Cross, if I see him again?"

"Nothing. Don't see him again."

"I wonder if you know how completely my whole outlook on life is changed by all this? I must find myself a new philosophy. Do you understand why that is so?"

"I think I do."

"How shall I start? My life has reached and passed a climax. Now I must begin again. How shall I go about it?"

"Quite simple. For a starter, why don't you marry me?"

Freddy Fletcher leaned back upon the red upholstered cushions and wielded a napkin conclusively. A waiter poured coffee. Elizabeth laughed, and her amused, deep eyes fell upon him appraisingly. He was an unexpected gentleman, was Mr. Frederick Fletcher.

"Why should I marry you?" she asked, critically.

"For no particular reason. I love you. You'll probably fall in love with me as soon as you get over the recent unpleasantness. I'm rich, sound in mind and limb. I'm not particularly a 'home body,' but I can assure you I'll not be boring. I like to go here and there and see this and that. You're practically bound to marry

199

some one within the next few months.
You couldn't do better than marry me.
It needn't, of course, be a permanent
arrangement."

Elizabeth stirred her coffee while her
heart beat with a curious excitement.
She seemed to see her tottering "great
adventure" reinstated in a new guise.
And she felt a very warm stirring of her
ready emotions toward the calm, rather
insolent young man beside her.

"How old are you?" she asked, inconsequentially.

"Thirty-four. I'll have a blank with
additional statistics drawn up for you tomorrow."

"You don't think the proposition a bit
premature?"

"I most certainly do. I don't expect
you to make up your mind for some days
—even weeks. But I can't help favoring
the plan, and I can't see any reason on
earth why I shouldn't point out to you
its obvious advantages. I don't, of course,
expect any answer—certainly not for
some time. In fact, I'd much rather not

have one. It is never good for the morale to be refused what one asks—even by a woman."

Elizabeth took a cigarette from a tortoise-shell case. For a few moments she was silent. Then she looked directly at him with her lazy, smiling eyes.

"I'm afraid I must disappoint you. I have decided to give you my answer now."

"Yes?" said Freddy Fletcher, his coffee cup motionless in his hand.

"I think your proposition an excellent one, ably presented. I'll marry you with pleasure."

"Humph!" commented Mr. Fletcher, putting the coffee cup to his lips. She was the kind of girl, he reflected, who would stake her life on a moment's impulse. Elizabeth went on, her poise completely restored.

"I saw a perfectly marvelous looking square diamond in Cartier's window, the other day," she suggested, amiably. "Aren't rings often used in connection with engagements?"

"Humph!" continued Mr. Frederick Fletcher, amply. He smiled a quiet, inward smile at the prospect of broaching the news to Willoughby Quimby.

CHAPTER 21.

Another Proposition. And Lucille Takes Pleasure in Being Kissed.

CAPTAIN THOMAS STIRLING, of the British Embassy, had meanwhile applied himself assiduously to an assault upon the warm young heart of Lucille Grosvenor. He had always looked upon himself as a confirmed bachelor. He had always vowed, with unwonted solemnity, that he would sooner live in a dry country than marry. But, as he now pointed out with eloquence, what the devil was he to do? The fates, said Captain Stirling, had decreed that he should wed Lucille. Who was he to gainsay the three sisters? It was conveyed to him that the girl, too, might be permitted a voice in the matter. He only looked perplexed. It being an already definitely established fact that he was to marry her, he failed to understand how she could help marrying him. Had he consulted her on the subject of the proposed step? He had. And she had answered—what? She had, proclaimed Captain Stirling triumphantly, answered that she was very flattered, that she adored to be loved, that she hoped he would go on loving her and proposing to her, that you never could tell, that she would love to have lunch with him at the Cascades, that she liked orchids,—yes, the pretty, expensive ones, —that she wasn't doing a thing that night and wasn't Maurice at the Jardin now?

So Tommy Stirling danced a cheerful, confident attendance, and Lucille was firmly convinced that she was being very clever about keeping him attached to her as an ever agreeable and docile escort. As to marrying him—that was another matter! Perhaps, some day, it might be fun to get engaged. But, to marry! When there were so many nice boys in the world? The over-sized brown eyes were wide with incredulity at the mere notion of an intrusion of matrimony on her terpsichorean youth.

The assurance of Captain Stirling, however, his calm assumption of ultimate victory, began to alarm Lucille. She resolved to take him down a peg. A plan occurred to her—one which she had employed with considerable success upon the callow youth of New York ballrooms. She resolved to lead Tommy on until he should try to kiss her. Then she felt that the icy weight of her rebuke would crush him to his proper place as an abject aspirant to her favors. The idea filled her with a gentle warmth of anticipation, and she went about it without delay.

The opportunity came one evening in the Bois. Tommy Stirling had stopped his car where a hot summer sunset poured a torrent of crimson fire down a narrow vista among the trees. They sat silent for a while and Lucille brought her face gently into a menacing proximity to his own. He looked with his cheerful gray eyes into the upturned

brown ones. Lucille smiled a little, her
lips parted. She began to be a little
piqued. No one else in her experience
had been able for so long to delay an attempt at amorous theft. She relaxed her
vigilance for a moment, and found herself suddenly swept against Tommy's
hard chest, felt his lips, no longer laughing now, very tightly pressed against hers,
felt his right arm around her shoulders
while his left caressed her cheek and the
little tendrils of brown hair beneath her
hat.

Lucille gasped, struggled, stamped her
foot, then was suddenly quiet. It was
rather nice, she thought. And, after all,
she couldn't get away. It wasn't as
though she wanted to be kissed. When
he let her go would be time enough to
protest. And she had never been so
pleasantly kissed in her whole life! She
wriggled a little, this time in pleasure,
and her eyes closed. For a moment, she
lay, dreaming, savoring the exquisite
niceness of the kissing. Then, in a moment of distraction, Lucille utterly for-

got herself, flung both her arms around his neck and their osculation became suddenly mutual.

Five minutes later, her hat and hair readjusted, her confusion more or less subsided, lip-stick reapplied to her lips and duly removed from Captain Stirling's cheek, Lucille attempted to reassert her dignity.

"You are not," she announced sternly, "to regard this—unhappy episode—as in any sense a precedent."

"Why not? I expect to go on kissing you for the rest of my life," replied Tommy, amiably.

"Well I don't expect you to!"

"Of course you do! Kissing is one of the things husbands are expected to do to their wives."

"But you're not my husband."

"I will be."

"I won't—I absolutely won't be engaged yet," wailed Lucille dismally.

"All right. I don't care whether you're engaged or not, as long as it's clearly established that you're going to marry me."

Lucille relapsed into an aggrieved and unwonted silence.

CHAPTER 22.

A Shadow Darkens the Horizon.

MR. QUIMBY felt himself miscast for the rôle into which he had been thrust. Irate parenthood was not an attitude to which his proclivities or the tradition of his tolerant past could be expected to lend themselves. He was prepared academically to acknowledge a certain unwisdom in Elizabeth's recent indiscretion. But of how or when or why he was to effect a remedy after the fact he knew not. Discipline, chastisement, he constitutionally regarded with supreme abhorrence. He had learned, at length and at some cost, the futility of counsel. Also, he had somewhat more than a doubt—even with the tolerant coloring of time—as to the security of his own position during the episode. The glass of his

own house was so fragile that he hesitated
long before even choosing of the stones
at his feet.

So Mr. Quimby's mental conflict en-
dured for three days and the upshot of
it all was that neither then nor at any
other time was the excursion to Chartres
mentioned between father and daughter.
Perhaps it was just as well so. In any
case, Mr. Quimby became quickly resigned to a discreet and knowing reticence—began indeed to regard himself as
a quite unusually wise and forbearing
parent. The inconsequentiality of which
Willoughby Quimby had made something of a categorical imperative was its
own reward. His positive refusal to fur-
row his brow left no channel for the
melancholic humor.

On the other hand, reflected Willoughby Quimby as he watched the driz-
zle on his window panes and the bubbles
in his brandy and soda, one conviction
he was being compelled to accept. A
daughter was a regrettably incomplete
gift without a supplementary mother.

The same might be said, he pursued, reviewing the earlier years of his marital life, some twenty years before, of a mother without a daughter. He wondered, inconsequentially, if his wife, even, would not have been supportable once Elizabeth had become something more than an array of unmotivated limbs equipped with irrepressible vocal apparatus. The reflection gave him pause. There were times when he would almost like to see his wife—from a position of security, be it understood, with an avenue of retreat carefully secured. But the notion was not a lasting one. After all, Mr. Quimby was not of an adventurous cast of mind. Any contact with the erstwhile Mrs. Quimby savored rather too much of the spectacular. He shuddered and looked apprehensively about. Flaming visions of a Xantippe-ridden eight years reeled across his mind. A terrible woman—terrible! Mr. Quimby took another sip of his brandy and soda, lit another cigarette and sank comfortably back in his easy chair. He picked up the recently delivered *Paris Times* and frowned at a knock at his door.

"Entrez, damn you!"

"Monsieur Quimby," the face of Joe resembled a landscape wracked with the earthquakes of centuries; "Monsieur Quimby—there is a lady. . . ."

"Well? What does she want?"

"She asks to be permitted to see Monsieur."

"Who is she?"

"She—Monsieur——!"

"Well—go on."

"It is—Madame Quimby, Monsieur."

The remaining fluid trickled from Mr. Quimby's overturned glass.

"My wife?"

"Oui, Monsieur."

CHAPTER 23.

Presenting a Woman of Some Importance.

MRS. WILLOUGBY QUIMBY'S entrance into a room was not unlike that of a knife into cheese or a razor into the chin. She was a long, keen woman. Actually, she found it unnecessary to stoop in the doorway, but such was nevertheless the impression conveyed by her spectacular slenderness and by a slight forward bend near her lofty summit. Her eyes were adorned with thick plates of opaque glass firmly attached to her nose by strong gold. Through the glass her gaze launched itself, a penetrating, darting forerunner of her coming.

"I shall have tea, Willoughby," she pronounced in a firm, not displeasing voice. "Also a cigarette, one of your

213

most agreeable smiles, a chair, and news
of my cub. I do hope it won't be good
news or bad tea."

Mr. Quimby, with the suavest of smiles
and cold horror in his heart, gestured his
recent wife to a chair.

"My dear, I can give you every assurance as to the quality of my tea. I rarely
touch it, so it is for the exacting palate
of my cook that it is brewed. As to your
—forgive me, *our* daughter, you may be
completely at ease. There is no good
news and a compensating weight of all
that is most reprehensible and depressing. But first let us talk of ourselves!
How have you been, how much have you
longed for your Willoughby's light step
on the stair, why have you come here?"

"I wonder if I've aged as much as you?
Or even half as much?" irrelevantly rejoined the newcomer.

"The answer, ex-beloved, is not even
obscure. You are ageless—the eternal
woman—Cleopatra, Helen, Lilith. I
see in you today that same majestic
enigma whose hot water-bottle it used to

be my inexpressible pleasure to load—
oh, how many, many years ago! But I,
too, have presented you with an interrogation. Why are you here?"

"Don't you know me well enough yet
to know that *I* don't *even* know why I'm
anywhere?" snapped Mrs. Quimby,
angrily manipulating a cigarette case.
Then, contradictorily, "I'm here because
I changed my mind. No daughter should
be trusted with a father. I have come to
do what I can to snatch the child out of
the fire before she becomes a cinder."

The entrance of Joseph caused a temporary distraction. Mr. Quimby ordered tea, and rum.

Mrs. Quimby leaped nervously to her
feet and began stalking up and down the
room, her eyes hot and bright behind the
thick pebbles of her pince-nez? Hers was
a dominant, impressive figure, with the
long, urgent limbs and the slightly bowed
shoulders. Suddenly she whirled on her
beaming husband, bent over his chair till
her sharp nose almost touched his suddenly solemn countenance.

215

"Damn it!" she snapped furiously.
"Tell me something. Tell me what's
happened to the obscene little angel—
quick and let's have done with it!"

Mr. Quimby was very pale and very
much alarmed. The situation aroused a
warm glow of reminiscence, carried him
back to the uneasy days of his matri-
monial misadventures. Also it turned his
heart to water. He tugged frantically at
his hair, he fidgeted, and his unimportant
eyes sought for refuge where he knew
of old there was none. Finally with a
deep sigh he became a hero.

"Our daughter," he remarked in the
coolest of tones, "is already, to continue
your expressive metaphor, already little
more than a smudge of soot. Let me
enumerate a few of her major exploits:
She is no longer a maid. She has had a
prolonged and very complete affair with
a gentleman whose experience and dis-
repute are both unlimited. She is, further, engaged to be married to one who
is—need I say more than that he is one
of my friends? With him, I anticipate

that she will enjoy perhaps several
months of complete happiness. I have
whole-heartedly given the match my paternal sanction."

Mr. Quimby's infrequent muscles con-
tracted in an impulse of terror. Almost,
he threw up his hand as though to ward
off a blow.

But his former mate was not a woman
of predictable moods. Slowly she stepped
back, her eyes unwontedly quiet. Before
this cataclysmic revelation she was
speechless. What was there to say, after
all? So Mrs. Quimby sat down very
quietly, watched Joseph set the tea-table,
and addressed her companion very
quietly.

"Suppose, Willoughby, we talk of
Paris? I haven't been here in years.
Who is here and what are they doing
and can I persuade you to take a dash
of tea in your rum? Before we begin,
though, shall we all plan to dine tomorrow night at Madrid? We all have so
very much to talk over."

"*Who* all?" demanded Willoughby

Quimby, with fear in his heart. His wife was very terrible when she was so calm and kindly.

"Why you, of course, dear—and Elizabeth, and our future son-in-law—and, if you think necessary, the premature corespondent—and anyone else you think would help to make it a nice party. If you have any particular mistress or mistresses, for example?"

Mr. Quimby groaned and poured very much rum into his cup.

CHAPTER 24.

Wherein Mr. Quimby Dreams an Ancient Dream.

THE Chateau de Madrid presented as usual the appearance of a somewhat overwrought garden party. Very expensive cars swept in amongst the tables and deposited very expensive women expensively adorned with gems and escorts. Nimble couples leaped and pranced and floundered and even danced in the allotted space. A haze of blue light made a sort of luminous shadow among the tall trees, while across the tables and the dance floor other expensive automobiles could be seen to slip noiselessly through the elfin lights. White and elusive in the magic atmosphere, the building itself became a palace in some artificial fairyland of the twentieth century.

Mr. Quimby, to whose peace of mind the stimulating wares of Dan had loaned no small support, was yet not wholly at his ease. His troubled gaze wandered across the table to where she who had once been his own was continuously devoting herself to the herculean labor of eliciting words from the wordless Freddy Fletcher on her right. Mr. Fletcher was distinctly heard on no less than two occasions during the meal, to vouchsafe an affable and meaningful "Yes?"

On Mr. Quimby's right he found little support or consolation in an equally laconical and sulky daughter. On his left lay only pitfalls and humiliation in the person of Miss Grosvenor, whose conversation was irrationally but wholly directed at one Thomas Stirling, opposite her. The latter couple Mr. Quimby had asked quite specifically because, while completely in touch with the existing situation, they might nevertheless be expected to clear the air of prospective thunders.

So Mr. Quimby was left pretty largely

to give himself to the enjoyment of his
food, to the repeated drainage of his wine
glass, to a mildly interested contemplation of the scene of opulent festivity before him. He was ironically amused to
see Conway Cross sitting *tête à tête* with
an unknown beauty, across the dance
floor. He stole a glance at Elizabeth.
She seemed unaware of the presence of
her former friend. Several acquaintances entered; others left. Mr. Quimby
greeted them all with carefully gradu-
ated cordiality—varying from a cheerful
grin or a nod to the most elaborate of
bows.

Suddenly the vagrant gaze became in-
explicitly fixed. Mr. Quimby could
rarely be said to look dumbfounded—
superficially, that is. But the fork he
had been in the act of raising, extraordinarily never reached his mouth. Instead,
he replaced it with meticulous precision,
with elaborate tranquility, upon his plate.
And his eyes did not shift.

Finally, Mr. Quimby started, drained
his glass with a hand that perhaps trem-

bled a shade, and his fingers slowly closed
on the sparse locks of his hair. Yet there
had been very little to awaken that intent
look, that indefinable indication that Mr.
Quimby's heart had quickened suddenly.
The focus of his vision fell on only one
person,—a woman of perhaps forty-five
summers. She was not a conspicuous
person, physically. Perhaps her most
notable features were a strikingly courageous evening gown, triumphant in its
judicious daring, a figure with which the
gods in coöperation with modern science
had dealt kindly, a face frankly and
boldly the debtor to a score of phials, of
pencils and of boxes, which yet possessed the inimitable grace of charm,
which may neither be isolated nor defined. A woman who had known and
seen much, yet a woman whose significance was not apparently more than that
of many another in that same gathering.

But Mr. Quimby, as he looked at her,
was thinking only a little of her. He
was dreaming a very old dream, and it
was not the first time that he had

dreamed it. And here is the dream that Willoughby Quimby was dreaming:

They were very young, the boy and girl who sat without speaking in an extremely pleasant room. They looked the younger for the fresh sorrow and pain on unaccustomed brows, for the uncertain, nervous twitching of young fingers, for their probable indifference to the cool fragrance entering by the long French windows and the green sweep of lawn and graveled drive down to a winding stream and a shaded bridge.

"Why did you come today, Will?" she asked him in a tiny voice. "There is nothing more to say. And so many things ended so completely—last night."

The boy twined his fingers spasmodically in the thick tangle of fair hair on his head and snatched a cigarette from his mouth with his trembling other hand.

"No, dear—you're terribly, terribly wrong! There's everything to say—and last night was not the end—it was a whole set of new beginnings. What do you ex-

223

pect, Caroline dear? We can't always go on this way without at least a difference of opinion—without——"

"We can't go on this way at all, Will. We should never have tried. We're too young and we're not strong enough. Oh, I don't mean that last night has any significance in itself. But it has dulled the keen edge of something very sharp and beautiful. And don't think for a minute that I'm reproaching you in the accepted way. I don't care a hang that you've made a 'ruined woman' of me. I've money enough, brains enough. If my life as I had dreamed it has been taken from me, I can make for myself a new life—perhaps even a new memory."

"Caroline!" he exclaimed, seizing her hand. "Don't talk like a baby. Come along, instead, and we'll get married. Then we can look on the last three months as no more than the preface to a beautiful book. We can——"

He stopped, because she had turned her eyes upon him and they were full of pity and a little anger.

"We can do nothing, Will. I wouldn't marry you today if my life depended on it. Marriage between us—now—would be like a peculiarly Chinese mode of mental torture. Thanks—I don't want to be made an honest woman. Goodby, Will."

He let her hand fall and they looked at each other for a moment. Then, because he never knew what to do at critical moments, young Willoughby Quimby walked out through the French window, down the graveled drive toward the stream. He looked back very furtively and quickly from the bottom of the hill at his happiness in the form of a very small white cottage with a green roof and rambling roses and green shutters— a very ordinary and very agreeable cottage.

In the pleasant little room the smoke of his cigarette had been almost completely dissipated by the light air, and the girl was not weeping, but stood very straight and still, thinking hard. It was

very probable that those two had loved
each other—a little.

That is the end of Mr. Willoughby
Quimby's slight dream, which he
dreamed in the Chateau de Madrid on
a certain Autumn evening.

Mr. Quimby did not yet address the
lady at the near-by table. Instead he
bowed his head wearily over his plate
and smiled, as though his dream held an
unaccustomed morsel for his rumination.
He was not conversationally moved.

In time the object of Mr. Quimby's
attention arose with a laugh trained to a
high pitch of exuberance and made her
way, accompanied by her somewhat
over-emphasized companions, toward a
waiting limousine. Mr. Quimby, with
low-voiced apology, followed. His wife,
her gaze thrusting after him, observed his
suave salutation of the lady, observed her
inquiring turn, the sharp surprise and
the sudden pain of her recognition; observed the gracious gesture of Mr. Quimby's explanations, of their subsequent

understanding, of their delayed fare-
wells. And the smile of Mrs. Quimby
bore an ironic implication which the
silent Mr. Fletcher did not fail to
remark.

But Mr. Quimby did not comment
upon his encounter when he again took
his seat between his disconsolate daughter and his eager friend. On the face of
her former help-mate Mrs. Quimby perceived an unwonted twist of the hand of
Time, and she, who knew him so much
better than she would, might have bar-
tered her happiness (as, indeed she once
did) to erase those new lines from a sag-
ging cheek.

CHAPTER 25.

Mr. Quimby Explores a New Path to Regeneration.

A TEA-TABLE in the shaded court of the Ritz was the scene of the next episode in the spiritual Odyssey of Willoughby Quimby. He sat in all the perfection of his studied attire, smiling the futile smile of perfect poise, accompanying the inanities of practiced conversation with the most accepted postures of his cup and spoon and toast. She leaned back with her shrewd and rather beautiful eyes amusedly upon him, aiding him not at all in his admirable conduct of a difficult occasion.

"I am," Mr. Quimby was saying, "of the revolutionary opinion that more than half of the people here do *not* come to 'see and be seen.' It would, in fact, not at all surprise me if very many of us are here quite simply because it is one of the pleasantest places in the entire world to obtain nourishment and the mild stimulus of tea and talk at a particularly barren time of the day."

"Will," his companion at length chose to take part in the conversation. "It is strange, isn't it, that we have not seen each other for so many years? Not strange that we have at length come together, but that we have not done so long ago."

"The world," mused Willoughby Quimby, "is a large place, after all, isn't it?"

He was ignored.

"I think," she went on, "that our love was the last important thing that ever happened to me—and probably to you."

"Isn't it unfair to both of us to call our adolescent fevers 'love'? Isn't it, as a matter of fact, unfair to call anything love?"

"I have heard a number of definitions of love," she answered, indifferently.

"They were all rather silly. I suppose 'adolescent fever' is the best of the lot."

They relapsed into their tea-cups and silence for a moment, before Willoughby Quimby answered.

"I am not at all sure," said he, "that any Paris *cocotte* wouldn't have just as good a definition."

She yawned a little.

"One may at least," she rejoined languidly, "be permitted to choose one's definitions of love. What is your choice?"

"Tea for two at the Ritz!" came gallantly from Mr. Quimby.

And again they were silent.

But the following morning, in the breakfast sunlight of Caroline Nash's apartment, Mr. Quimby was not at all silent. With his habitual gay volubility he outlined plans, he discussed auto routes, he put new and astonishing touches into the fair landscape of their future. There was talk of much motoring, of this and that quaint *auberge,* of this and that dazzling resort. A suite at the Villa d'Este, at the Negresco in Nice, at the Excelsior at the Lido, with the attendant sunshine of the South, figured prominently. And the alternatives were legion—a particular Villa on the slopes of Florence, a similar fairy palace in the white sunlight near Cannes, all these things brought a bright, pathetic light into the pale blue of Mr. Quimby's eyes.

The woman, pink and marvelously fresh in a negligible negligee, smiled upon him with an amusement that was almost wholly affectionate. Paris had been a new field for the magic of her charm, that white sorcery the exercise of which had been for many years distorted into a labor and a long weariness. She had seen him grow before her eyes, had seen new wine poured into the old vessel of his emotions. They had caught together a lingering fragrance of their united youth.

At last Mr. Quimby finished his coffee and brandy and his cigarette, and took his reluctant leave.

"The cold hand of Responsibility is on my shoulder," he announced. "I must to my daughter to assure her that my absence for the night was due to the urgence of my vocational duties. I must to my ex-spouse to assure her of my continued devotion to her interests. I must to the money-changers to make ready the way for my hegira. So, Caroline, I salute you and leave you—for the nonce."

"And you will be here?"

"Tomorrow morning at ten—without fail. And then—a *vita nueva* for us both!"

"I shan't see you before?"

"Alas! The cares of family—the domestic yoke!"

"Then—Goodby."

"*Au revoir!*"

So departed the jubilant Willoughby Quimby.

CHAPTER 26.

But Willoughby Quimby Persists in Being the Creature of His Destiny.

THAT night Willoughby Quimby sat long but temperately over his beer at the Deux Maggots. His mood was far other than it had been on that other moonlit evening when he had first assailed the impregnable bastions of youth. Lucille was tonight the haziest of memories. To her he left her untutored exuberances, her raptures and her superlatives; to her— was "dashing" the word?—young suitor; to her a world which he had been a superannuated fool to covet and a bigger fool to anticipate achievement of.

As for him, Willoughby Quimby, he had found the veritable elixir, the authentic fount. He, grizzled and debauched and inactive, had succeeded in

233

turning back the clock, in erasing the wasted middle years, in attaining a vanquishing continuity between the old dream of young love and the young dream of his latest love. All that had gone between had no more meaning than the leaves that rustled on the boulevard trees. All that gave his life significance was embodied in the one imperious name —Caroline!

Mr. Quimby drank deep of his *demiblonde*. Mr. Quimby inhaled the spicy air of a cool evening, laden with the acrid breaths of a thousand panting motors. Mr. Quimby was ecstatic. That was it —he was exercising long-disused emotions, exercising them with a scope and a cunning that unscorched youth might never know. Mr. Quimby felt that at last he had justified his life through perfect conduct of it, coming to its ultimate fruit in one of the perfect loves of the ages.

A strange epic, this romance of his, reflected Willoughby Quimby. Here were two who had met in the first fresh gleam of their youth, who had made of their meeting a torch to light their journey—and had parted to walk the dim ravines of life, to learn its bitter and its sweet, to bring the fruit of their experience and its teaching to carry on the old flambeau with disillusioned, certain step and the brave eye of infinite knowledge! Mr. Quimby was delighted with himself.

So, still delighted with himself, he arose and walked through the evening, down narrow shadowed streets to the Seine, and followed its bank in a high exaltation of spirit for some distance before he confided himself and his beatitude to a Citroen taxi and a corpulent driver. Followed a night-cap at his rooms, a last touch to his preparations for the journey of the morrow, and Mr. Quimby retired to his transfigured slumbers.

The morning found Willoughby Quimby not a little irritable, consequent upon his gentle awaking at the hands of a sympathetic Joseph. His first impulse was protest, his second to burrow under

the sheets and sleep again. From both
he was deterred by a vague, not unpleasant thrilling in his bosom. He felt indefinably that this day held in store
something singularly agreeable. Mr.
Quimby tugged at his hair, painfully dis-
entangled his intelligence from the enveloping gauzes of slumber, and, to the
intense confusion of Joseph, sat bolt up-
right.

At last he had it! Today was the day
of his emancipation. Today life took
on meaning. He was no longer to be
a tipsy wanderer from bar-room to cabaret. He was to redeem himself by the
supreme miracle of sophisticated and mature romance.

Mr. Quimby nearly effected the complete dislocation of Joseph's excessively
perturbable features. He was changed
to a model of energy. He paced the
room, he carved small wedge-shaped
morsels from his face with a safety razor,
he put things into his bag and took them
out again, he spilled his brandy flip, he
slipped in his bath and rent the air with

236

howls of pain. Despite the delay result-
ing from his inordinate haste, he was,
however, eventually dressed, packed,
adorned with a fresh gardenia. A slight
delay in the arrival of the car evoked
frantic 'phone calls to the garage.

At long last, Mr. Quimby was in the
car, the sun beamed auspiciously upon
him, and he was borne swiftly to his rendezvous.

On the way, Mr. Quimby reflected further on the voluptuous maturity of his
lady's charms, on the kindred subtlety of
her mental processes, on the splendid
scope of her outlook. At last, felt Mr.
Quimby, he had found the mate adapted
to his peculiar manners of mind and
conduct.

The car pulled up before the agreeable building in which his inamorata
made her nest. Mr. Quimby stepped out,
twirled his cane, entered. He manipu-
lated the lift, dispatched it again to its
ground floor resting place. With a beating heart, he awaited the answer to his
ring.

"Mme. Nash?" he inquired of the pretty maid who opened to him.

"Madame," said the maid with imperturbable brutality, "has not risen. Madame confided to me this note, which she begged me to place in the hands of M. Quimby."

Mr. Quimby tore open the note with trembling fingers. It read as follows:

"Dear Will:

I'm absolutely broken-hearted, but I'm afraid we must call off or, at least, postpone, our little trip. I can't possibly explain everything until I see you but perhaps you'll understand when I tell you that I promised last night to marry Juan Bassanez. He is Argentinian, greasy, wealthy and nice. Perhaps you know him. Please, Willoughby dear, forgive me.

Love,

Caroline."

Mr. Quimby refolded the note, placed it back in its envelope, put the envelope

238

carefully in his pocket, nodded pleasantly to the maid, and walked thoughtfully down the three flights of stairs to his waiting car. It must be acknowledged that he blinked imperceptibly when he caught sight of the luggage strapped on the rear of the car.

CHAPTER 27.

Containing the Mature Contemplation of Mr. Willoughby Quimby at a Critical Period.

HAVING treated himself to a drive in the Bois, Mr. Quimby, his thoughts by this time somewhat cleared, saw but one course open to him. He repaired to Dan's for a philosophic brandy and soda. Dan, detecting with the unerring perception of his vocation that something was amiss, greeted Mr. Quimby sympathetically. He devoted all of his attention to the diversion of his depressed client. He indulged in not very satisfactory wheezes; he won a drink at poker dice, drank a spoonful of champagne in a tumbler of seltzer and changed ten francs for it; he related the current gossip of bibulous circles.

"Dan," confided Mr. Quimby gloomily, "a woman has repulsed my advances."

"The hussy!" was Dan's sufficient comment.

"She has preferred an Argentine."

"The perverted gold-digger!"

Drinking was resumed in silence. Dan put things in a glass, slapped a metallic cover upon the glass and handed the vessel to an assistant for shaking.

"Dan," asked Mr. Quimby thoughtfully, "have I ever appeared discontented with my lot in life?"

Dan weighed the matter gravely before replying. Then he shook his head.

"Only in the mornings, Mr. Quimby."

"Have I ever threatened to settle down to complacent domesticity?"

"I'm afraid not," sighed the bartender, —in his hours of ease the most domestic of parents.

So Mr. Quimby finished his brandy and soda and left the place. Rejecting a taxi proffered by the zealous doorman, Mr. Quimby walked. He walked for a very long time, not particularly noting

241

the way of his walking. Finding himself at length at the Pont Neuf, he became conscious of a very great deal of pain in his feet and a great deal of weariness in his legs.

But he had come no nearer to putting his mental house in order. The most he could attain to was an unreasoning condemnation of his daughter. It was her coming which had first suggested this disquieting rebellion against the otherwise complacent idleness of his life. Why the devil, he reflected, should he be bothered making this wholly futile campaign for rejuvenescence? He had been happy before—why reach for stars which, he was fundamentally convinced, were not stars at all? He permitted himself a chuckle at the feeble failure of his attempts. He had chased his will-o'-the-wisp now three times—through the responsibility of paternity, the purity of naïve romance, the sophisticated illusion of mature love. And all that had resulted was ignoble defeat.

Mr. Quimby looked mournfully up at

the heroic equestrian shape of Henri
Quatre, gleaming under the high sun.
But he was less fortunate than Mr.
Locke's vagabond. The martial poten-
tate vouchsafed no sign, turned never an
inch his regal head. Mr. Quimby
groaned, made his way to a café on the
place St. Michel, indulged in a swart
picon citron. Again he lapsed into rev-
ery.

CHAPTER 28.

Wherein the Title of This Book is Sufficiently Justified.

THE eyes of Willoughby Quimby were fixed for a long time on a large dark blotch of moisture on the pavement, where a waiter had flung the remnant of a half-emptied carafe of water. He sipped his *apéritif* absently, and his pale gaze did not waver. Until at last there came across his face a curious light. Slowly his eyes were raised, passed unseeing away from the wet spot on the sidewalk, passed the curb, crept up the forms of passers-by and became unseeingly fixed upon a point midway up the side of a house across the square. Mr. Quimby's mouth opened a trifle and shut again. His right hand crept slowly to the fringe of grizzled hair under his felt hat.

244

Mr. Quimby had had his fifth intimation of renascense. Another great, redeeming idea had come to presage the transmutation of his existence, to give shining meaning to his life. Another road had opened to him, a path of escape from the treadmill of crapulous idleness.

He paid for his drink, hailed a taxi, and was borne on his rattling course to the Hotel Meurice, where the commanding Mrs. Quimby made her temporary home.

Due telephonic negotiations having been carried out and all preliminaries attended to, Mr. and Mrs. Quimby found themselves convivially ensconced at a detached table in the Ritz dining room. Mr. Quimby was at his best. His conversation rippled with a smooth affability that was irresistible. His anecdotes were incomparable, his epigrams flawlessly turned. He had a sharp tag of gossip for every one in the room. Mrs. Quimby eyed him suspiciously and said little. Patiently she awaited the subject which she was convinced he was to

245

broach, but whose nature she could not divine.

With a culminating sigh of satisfaction, Mr. Quimby, the fragrance of coffee in his nostrils, leaned back and devoted himself to the removal of a patrician band from a momentous cigar. Followed a silence while the flame of a match was fastidiously applied. And then spoke Mr. Quimby in this wise:

"My dear, I have something of grave import to communicate!"

"Communicate it then!" uncompromisingly snapped the lady.

Mr. Quimby filled the air with blue fragrance and then went on.

"The coming of Elizabeth, her influence upon me, my temporary responsibility for her welfare—all this has had upon me an effect at whose profundity I can only marvel."

"Huh!"

Mr. Quimby moved awkwardly. She was not an easy woman to talk to, he reflected, as so often he had reflected in the past.

"That effect," he continued, "has been magnified a thousand fold by—if you'll permit my putting it so—the renewal of my association with, my dear, your inspiring self." Mr. Quimby paused.

"Go on."

"Hmm. Well—as I say—I feel a new man. I have come at last to see the error of my way, and to ask your help in making of my contrition a redemption."

"What do you mean?" sharply.

"I mean—this," Mr. Quimby's tones were strained. "I mean that—well—in the first place—I mean—I have been agreeably—I'll not say 'surprised,' quite —to find that the old sentiment which I once cherished in respect to you, Florence, and which I have long thought extinct, is, as a matter of fact, a smoldering ember which nor time nor any of our superficial differences may extinguish. I am eager to believe that the same might be said with equal truth of your own feeling in regard to myself!"

"Huh."

247

"I am about to reform. I am about to stop drinking. I am anxious to work."

"Indeed!"

"In short, I am to be a new man. The effort required will be gigantic. I cannot bear the burden alone. I want your aid. In short, Florence, I want you to take me back!"

Mrs. Quimby stirred her coffee in thoughtful silence. Then, slowly she took a cigarette from a tortoise-shell case. Assiduously, Mr. Quimby leaned toward her with his silver lighter. He steadied his hand with an elbow on the table. Another long silence.

"Willoughby," at length remarked Mrs. Quimby, in a casual tone, "are you going to the races this afternoon?"

Mr. Quimby did not answer, and across his flabby features went a sudden flash of pain. Suddenly Mrs. Quimby put her hand on his arm and her pointed gaze softened.

"I'm sorry, Willoughby! That was unfair. But—all I can say is this:—

Thank you. But what you suggest is a little more than impossible."

"Why?" Mr. Quimby's voice was very low.

"Because, for one thing, I am to be married again in a month," the eyes sharpened again, defiantly.

"To whom?" He straightened suddenly.

"Does it matter?"

"I had heard nothing of it."

"I haven't bothered to tell any one!"

Mr. Quimby's mouth twisted into a shadow of his accustomed irony.

"Have you, my dear, bothered to tell the happy man himself?" he asked earnestly.

When they parted, a half-hour later, Mrs. Quimby stopped for a moment at the door of her hotel, watching the taxi that bore her rejected suitor. She laughed quietly, but it was not an unkindly laugh.

As for Mr. Quimby, he leaned back in the cab with a deep sigh, and then he laughed, too. It was a very wholesome laugh, this one, for Willoughby Quimby was laughing at himself. He stretched his arms as wide as the compass of the car permitted and felt, curiously, a new ease. One by one he had tried in vain every egress from the prison of his liberty, and now he was free again.

The taxi paused before the swinging doors of Dan's place, and Mr. Quimby entered. The place was almost vacant at this hour and Mr. Quimby went straight to the bar.

"Dry Martini, please, Dan," said Willoughby Quimby as he placed a contented foot upon the rail.

Afterword

BY MORRILL CODY

John A. M. Thomas, author of *Dry Martini,* was fresh out of Yale when he arrived in Paris in 1922. In college he had been chairman of the *Yale Literary Magazine,* winner of the Metcalf Prize for a dramatic essay, and it was generally considered that he was headed for a literary career. He planned to round out his formal education with studies at the Sorbonne and enrich his horizon by contact with the writers, artists, and bons vivants who were then escaping to Paris from Prohibition and the middle-class morality of America. As a "writer of promise" already endowed with a reasonable income for which no work was required, he could afford to take his time in absorbing the atmosphere of the City of Light.

But Jack Thomas did not rush to join the hungry intellectuals of the Left Bank. He doubtless felt himself above that. He preferred the romantic and decadent remains of the Edwardian era which he found on the Right Bank. The two were as different as blue and red (Left Bank), yet they managed to survive in the same city and even, at times, in direct contact with each other. Jack, for instance, lived on the Right Bank, frequented the bars and night spots around him, yet was anxious also to know the life of Montparnasse. He spent long hours in his study of both worlds, but in *Dry Martini* he expresses only the charm and the fantasy of the Edwardian. Although the novel was written long after that period of opulence and decadence had officially closed, the Edwardian style was far from forgotten. In the twenties there were still remnants of the glorious life of pre-World War I when servants, barmen, and mistresses (even wives) found it entirely natural to be devoted to "the master" and to find their own satisfaction in the reflection of his glory.

This was the world of Man, and especially the Englishman and his American imitator. Persons of other nationalities were "foreigners" and not to be trusted. To be a man-about-town of that era, one needed certain equipment, not the least of which was a bit of money to spend freely. A gentleman's gentleman was an essential, of course, that suave, educated, unassuming, graceful individual who managed the master's household, mixed the martinis, arranged the parties, sent out the invitations, kept records of the girl friends, and only took time off for himself to visit his aged aunt on alternate Sunday afternoons. He survives today only in certain detective fiction and in cartoon strips.

A mistress too was most important to the picture, the beautiful, gay creature who accompanied him to the races, the theatre, and the supper clubs, and then led him home to their happy little hideaway on the rue de Rivoli or the Avenue du Bois de Boulogne, as the Avenue Foch was then called. Traditionally the mistress was devoted, tolerant, and loving, but also, even at the height of Edwardianism, somewhat demanding. She did not mind being cooped up all day in the apartment with her devoted and gossipy maid, but in the evening she wanted to go out, *every* evening. The man-about-town, on the other hand, didn't necessarily desire to go abroad that often. He might prefer to have his dinner with friends where new feminine faces would permit his mind to wander momentarily at least from thoughts of the mistress waiting so impatiently elsewhere. Or perhaps the master merely wished to drink and dine alone with an old chum of war or university days in a quiet place where he would not be disturbed by the female voice. For the Londoner this meant his club where the steward anticipated his every need and was the confidant of every member. Paris, however, had no such clubs and this is how the bartender in certain establishments came to hold a position somewhat similar to that of the steward.

It is obvious that in his description of the "Garden of Allah" and "Dan, the bartender" Thomas had in mind the "back door" bar of the Ritz Hotel on the rue Cambon. Here Frank Meier, the famous "Frank" of the twenties, himself an escapee from the Hoffman House in New York, held sway as the friend and confidant of the serious English and American drinkers of the Right Bank.

The Ritz Bar was an establishment of considerably more complexity than Thomas's meager description portrays. In the first place it was two bars, one on either side of the street entrance. The one on the left had a solid, heavy door, and even when it was opened, it was almost impossible to see anyone on the inside. This was the men's bar and no feminine foot was permitted to cross its threshold. It was said that even the early morning "cleaning women" were men. At the back of the room was a massive oak bar with the customary brass footrail, and on the left was a partitioned inner sanctum where the customer could partake of nourishment other than liquids should he find himself reduced to such an extremity. He thus was saved the nuisance of having to walk that long long hall to the restaurant on the "front door" or Place Vendome side where he would be subject to scrutiny from—horrors!—females.

Not that the patrons of the Ritz all-male bar were antiwomen. Far from it, indeed. But a surfeit of girls at certain hours of the day or night often led to a desire to escape at other times to the splendid isolation of Frank's soothing establishment.

And then there was the other bar on the right hand side of the entrance hall, also managed by Frank, a room of equal size with double glass doors through which all the clients were plainly visible. This was known as the "steam room." Dotted with small tables, here was the domain where ladies could gather for tea or cocktails and *no man was admitted* unless he accompanied one of the female guests. As the result of this obviously unfair discrimination every young blood wanted to get in, wanted to be seen in this realm of the opposite sex. There were usually a half dozen men, young and old, hanging around the entrance, trying to catch the eye of a guest who would then signal to the custodian of the door that the gentleman in question was persona grata to her. Once seated at her table the lucky man could survey the crowd of ladies, perhaps be introduced to one or two, and be given the honor of paying the bill when his acquaintance decided to move on.

Today no establishment in Paris has the animation

of the better known bars in the twenties. Their clients were largely English and American, though there was also a goodly sprinkling of sophisticated internationalists of French, Italian, and Central European background. They represented decadence at its best.

Of them all, the Ritz Bar was by far the leader. It stood for the majesty and indolence of the Right Bank as the Dome and Dingo personified the bohemianism and permissiveness of the Left Bank. With few exceptions the two rarely mixed. They even despised each other. Thomas gives a clear picture of the Right Bank scorn for the Left Bank in one chapter of this book. Left Bankers were equally voluble in their contempt for the effete, dressed-up snobs across the river. A true Left Banker never set foot on the Right Bank except to cash a check, for unfortunately there were no financial facilities in bohemia. When he did make such a foray, he grabbed his money and ran back home as fast as his legs would carry him.

The exceptions to this monomania were some of the foreign journalists whose professional duties required them to inhabit both banks of the Seine and those writers who had achieved sufficient material success to be able to buy the more formal Right Bank clothes and pay Frank for sustained drinking at the Ritz. Among these were F. Scott Fitzgerald, Louis Bromfield, and a little later Ernest Hemingway joined the habitués. One who was often present was Michael Arlen whose novel *The Green Hat* had put him in front rank. Erskine Gwynne, one of the Vanderbilts and publisher of *The Boulevardier,* a magazine which wrote the epitaph for the fading days of Edwardianism, was also a constant visitor to the Ritz Bar. Other, though less frequent, guests were Noel Coward who was busy satirizing the manners of the period in his kindly way, and also Somerset Maugham.

Here, among writers and men-about-town and gentlemen-in-relaxed-positions was Jack Thomas, observing, drinking, planning his book, a tall, thin, blond man with glasses. He had a slightly superior air about him and was always well behaved. He might have been a young professor on sabbatical.

"I remember him well," Monsieur Bertin, the present chief barman at the Ritz, said to me recently. "I was only an apprentice in those far-off days, but I remember Thomas particularly because he was always so kind and quiet. He was a good friend of Fitzgerald and Bromfield, and, I think, of Hemingway also. He came in every day. He was a fine man." And after a few moments thought he added, "But all men who drink are good persons."

To the bartender the "good person" is of course the

one who drinks regularly, pays promptly without ever asking for credit, and makes no trouble whether drunk or sober. Frank's customers were mostly very well behaved, but in any case he managed them with a remarkable mixture of firmness and kindness, the iron hand hidden in the softest possible velvet glove. If a client showed signs of succumbing to an overdose of alcohol, Frank would be right there helping him with his coat and murmuring "Your taxi is waiting, sir." Should the man protest that he hadn't ordered a taxi, Frank would express surprise, assure him that he had, and gently but surely propel him toward the door. How Frank always managed to have such a ready supply of taxis has always been a mystery to me.

It is significant that the only other person I have found who knew Jack Thomas well in those days is another bartender and this one a representative of the Left Bank. I refer to Jimmy Charters who now lives in London and at eighty has given up bartending. In the twenties Jimmy held a position in the Montparnasse world somewhat similar to that of Frank on the Right Bank. But instead of presiding over a particular establishment, Jimmy moved around from bar to bar taking his devoted clients with him. The Dingo is doubtless his best-known bar, but the Falstaff, Trois et As, and Sans Souci are also memorable. One of the less remembered was Parelli's on the rue Vavin, better known later as the College Inn. Here Jack Thomas and Jimmy became fast bar friends. A "bar friend" is one you know intimately when you are in the bar and barely recognize when you are not.

Jimmy remembers that Jack always dressed in dark (Right Bank) suits and that he was more dignified than his other customers. He often sat at the bar, talking to Jimmy and others in friendly fashion and keeping an eye out for the girls. He spent money freely, buying drinks for others, but never throwing it around. In the English edition of Jimmy's memoirs he mentions Thomas as a man "who always wanted what he coudn't get," and today he thinks that the basis for this cryptic remark was Jack's inability to hold the affections of any of the girls he met. Many were drawn to this generous and warm young man, but each in turn dropped him after the first round. Something of this kind is indicated in this book in the adventures of Mr. Quimby. Thomas would take these rebuffs in his stride and return to the bar where he would sometimes sit for hours at a time. Jimmy remarks that he even ate Parelli's Italian meals which he still looks upon as an act of extreme devotion. When Jimmy moved from Parelli's to another bar, Jack Thomas, unlike his other customers, did not follow and Jimmy never saw him again.

DRY MARTINI

As a novel *Dry Martini* captures the spirit of high
romance that marked the belle époque in France and
the Edwardian period in Britain, for both countries the
waning years of undisputed colonialism and privilege
for the moneyed classes over the less fortunate. While
democratic influences were strong on paper and in the
speeches of a few politicians, these same "less fortu-
nates" were content for the moment with the considerable gains they had achieved in their standard of living
and in their personal freedoms. Meanwhile the notables
of the upper classes, combined with the not incon-
siderable remnants of the nobility, continued to exercise their prerogatives as though no social upheaval had
occurred. Thomas portrays one phase of this remarkable
time with deadly accuracy, this world of the courtly
bow, intrigue, secrets everyone knew, and inevitable
good manners. It was a society artificial yet full of
charm, dishonest yet momentarily sincere, in which the
cad and the fallen woman mixed with people of the
highest moral principles.

Ah Virtue! It shone brighter than a star, its pure
light visible to all. But when the point of honor had
been established and dealt with, the beautiful people
returned to their witty indolence and superficial dalliance
without a qualm.

Thomas's stylized prose fits the atmosphere of this

period better, in some ways, than the oversophisticated phrases of Noel Coward in such theatre pieces as *Nude with Violin* where the farce of a gentleman's gentleman outplays the reality of a period that today is looked back upon more and more with genuine warmth and nostalgia. *Dry Martini,* though written perhaps with tongue in cheek, is nevertheless a serious effort to portray the real world of its time. The sentences and the story flow with an ease which rings true to life. The situations and the descriptions are entirely readable, such as the image of the Hotel Grande Monarche in Chartres which has hardly changed today and is still a romantic inn for many a couple with an eye for the past.

Thomas spent three years in Paris. Bertin believes that he left in early 1925 at a point when the influx of tourists was beginning to dim the euphoria of the original escape to Edwardian or bohemian paradise. We next hear of Jack in New York where he married Josephine Scott in April 1925 and, after an extended honeymoon in Europe, he tried to settle down to a career as a writer and New York socialite. *Dry Martini* was published in 1926 and was subsequently made into a motion picture. He had a promising future, everyone said.

This was the era of the speakeasy and Thomas soon found himself absorbed in research for his next book among the habitués of the bars of Manhattan. According to Lucius Beebe, he was working on a history of 58th Street from the East River to the Hudson. He saw it as a typical cross-section of New York, as indeed it was, including in the same street the worlds of the very rich, the very poor, stage folk, gamblers, denizens of night life, criminals, and much more. It might have been a great book. Unfortunately, Jack only got as far as Dan Moriarty's place at 216 East 58th and thereafter made it his drinking headquarters. It is perhaps due to his friendship with Moriarty that he chose "Dan" as the name of the bartender in this book.

But the moderation for which Jack was known in the bars in Paris began to desert him in Manhattan. The effects on his health and personal life soon became noticeable. After a couple of years his marriage began to fall apart and by 1930 he was divorced. Finally, in 1932, John A. M. Thomas died of acute chronic alcoholism in a mid-town hotel, a sad victim of the martinis he has so lauded in this entertaining book.

Textual Note: The text of *Dry Martini* published here is a photo-offset reprint of the first printing (New York: Doran, 1926). The so-called "movie edition" (New York: Grosset & Dunlop, 1928) was a reprint of the first edition. No emendations have been made in the text.   M. J. B.